Praise for *New York Times*
and *USA TODAY* bestselling author

BRENDA
JACKSON

"Brenda Jackson writes romance that sizzles and
characters you fall in love with."
—*New York Times* and *USA TODAY* bestselling author
Lori Foster

"Jackson's trademark ability to weave multiple
characters and side stories together makes shocking
truths all the more exciting."
—*Publishers Weekly*

"There is no getting away from the sex appeal
and charm of Jackson's Westmoreland family."
—*RT Book Reviews* on *Feeling the Heat*

"Jackson's characters are wonderful, strong, colorful
and hot enough to burn the pages."
—*RT Book Reviews* on *Westmoreland's Way*

"The kind of sizzling, heart-tugging story Brenda
Jackson is famous for."
—*RT Book Reviews* on *Spencer's Forbidden Passion*

"This is entertainment at its best."
—*RT Book Reviews* on *Star of His Heart*

Dear Reader,

It is hard to believe that we are celebrating the tenth anniversary of the Westmorelands. It seemed like it was only yesterday when I introduced you to Delaney and her five brothers. I knew by the time I wrote Thorn's story that I just had to tell you about their cousins. Now twenty-three books later, we are still going strong.

It has been an adventure and I appreciate sharing it with you. Thank you. I've gotten your emails and snail mails letting me know how much you adore those Westmoreland men and I appreciate hearing from you. Each Westmoreland—male or female—is unique and the way love takes control of their hearts is both heartwarming and breathtaking.

In this story, Riley Westmoreland is willing to take a chance on love with a woman who has a past she'd rather not deal with. But this Westmoreland man shows her that true love can conquer all.

I hope you enjoy this story about Riley Westmoreland and Alpha Blake.

Happy reading!

Brenda Jackson

BRENDA JACKSON

ONE WINTER'S NIGHT

HARLEQUIN®
entertain, enrich, inspire™

To the love of my life, Gerald Jackson, Sr.

Happy holidays to all my family, friends and dedicated readers.

A very special thank you to event planners extraordinaire—
Shikara Linsy, Sandra Sutton, Tammy Griffin, and Tracy Hale.
My interview with you regarding the life of an event planner and
your patience in answering all of my questions was most appreciated.

Pleasant words are a honeycomb,
sweet to the soul and healing to the bones.
—*Proverbs,* 16:24

ISBN-13: 978-0-373-73210-4

ONE WINTER'S NIGHT

Copyright © 2012 by Brenda Streater Jackson

Recycling programs
for this product may
not exist in your area.

www.Harlequin.com

Printed in U.S.A.

BRENDA JACKSON

is a die "heart" romantic who married her childhood sweetheart and still proudly wears the "going steady" ring he gave her when she was fifteen. Because she believes in the power of love, Brenda's stories always have happy endings. In her real-life love story, Brenda and her husband of forty years live in Jacksonville, Florida, and have two sons.

A *New York Times* bestselling author of more than seventy-five romance titles, Brenda is a recent retiree who now divides her time between family, writing and traveling with Gerald. You may write Brenda at P.O. Box 28267, Jacksonville, Florida 32226, by email at WriterBJackson@aol.com or visit her website at www.brendajackson.net.

THE DENVER WESTMORELAND FAMILY TREE

Raphel and Gemma Westmoreland

Stern Westmoreland (Paula Bailey)

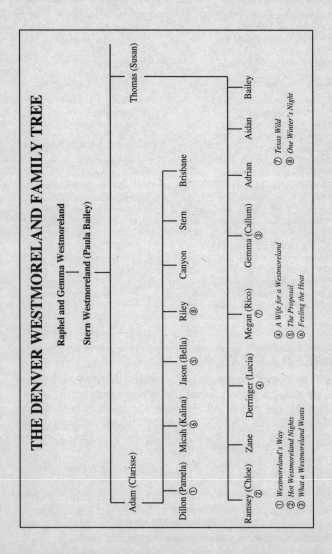

Thomas (Susan)

Adam (Clarisse)

Dillon (Pamela) ①

Micah (Kalina) ⑥

Jason (Bella) ⑤

Riley ⑧

Canyon

Stern

Brisbane

Ramsey (Chloe) ②

Zane

Derringer (Lucia) ④

Megan (Rico) ⑦

Gemma (Callum) ③

Adrian

Aidan

Bailey

① *Westmoreland's Way*
② *Hot Westmoreland Nights*
③ *What a Westmoreland Wants*

④ *A Wife for a Westmoreland*
⑤ *The Proposal*
⑥ *Feeling the Heat*

⑦ *Texas Wild*
⑧ *One Winter's Night*

One

A blistering cold day in early November

It had snowed overnight and a thick white blanket seemed to cover the land as far as the eye could see. The Denver weather report said the temperature would drop to ten below by midday and would stay that way through most of the night. It was the kind of cold you could feel deep in your bones, the kind where your breath practically froze upon exhale.

He loved it.

Riley Westmoreland opened the door to his truck and, before getting inside, paused to take in the land he owned. *Riley's Station* was the name he'd given his one-hundred-acre spread seven years ago, on his twenty-fifth birthday. He had designed the ranch house himself and had helped in the building of it, proudly hammering the first nail into the lumber. He was mighty pleased with the massive two-story structure that sat smack in the center of his snow-covered land.

He was probably the only one in his family who welcomed

the snowstorms each year. He thought the snow was what made Denver the perfect place to be in the winter and why his home had fireplaces in all five of the bedrooms, as well as in the living room and family room. There was nothing like curling up before a roaring fire or looking out the window to see the snowflakes fall from the sky, something he'd been fascinated with even as a child. He could recall being out in the thick snow with his brothers and cousins building snowmen. These days he enjoyed moving around the mountains on his snowmobile or going skiing in Aspen.

Riley got into the truck and after settling his body on the leather seat he snapped the seat belt in place. There really was no need for him to go into the office since he could work from home. But he had wanted to get out, breathe in the cold, fresh air and feel the chill in his bones. Besides, he did have an important appointment at noon.

Since his oldest brother, Dillon, had slowed down now that his wife, Pam, was close to her delivery date, a lot of the projects on Dillon's plate at their family-owned business, Blue Ridge Land Management, fell on Riley's shoulders since he was the next man in charge of the Fortune 500 company. The next thing on the agenda was the planning of the employees' holiday party next month.

The event planner that had handled their social functions for the past ten years had retired and before Riley had taken over the project, Dillon had hired Imagine, a local event planning company that opened in town less than a year ago. The owner of Imagine, a woman by the name of Alpha Blake, had put together a charity event that Dillon's wife, Pam, had attended over the summer. Pam had been so impressed with all the detailed work Imagine had done that she passed the woman's name to Dillon. As far as Riley was concerned, you couldn't come any more highly recommended than that. Dillon trusted his wife's judgment in all things.

Riley was about to start the ignition when his cell phone buzzed. He pulled the phone off his side belt. "Yes?"

"Mr. Westmoreland?"

He lifted a brow, not recognizing the ultrarich, feminine voice but definitely liking how it sounded. He figured this had to be a business call since none of the women he dated would refer to him as "Mr. Westmoreland."

"Yes, this is Riley Westmoreland. How can I help you?"

"This is Alpha Blake. We have a noon appointment at your office, but I have a flat tire and had to pull off to the side of the road. Unfortunately, I'm going to be late."

He nodded. "Have you called for road service?"

"Yes, and they said they should be here in less than thirty minutes."

Don't count on it, he thought, knowing how slow road service could be this time of the year. "Where's your location, Ms. Blake?"

"I'm on Winterberry Road, about a mile from the Edgewater intersection. There's a market not far away, but it didn't appear to be open when I drove past earlier."

"And chances are it won't be open today. Fred Martin owns that market and never opens the day after a bad snowstorm," he said.

He knew her exact location now. "Look, you're not far from where I am. I'll call my personal road service company to change your tire. In the meantime, I'll pick you up and we can do a lunch meeting at McKay's instead of meeting at my office, since McKay's is closer. And afterward, I can take you back to your car. The tire will be changed by then."

"I—I don't want to put you to any trouble."

"You won't. I know you and Dillon have gone over some ideas for the party, but since I'll be handling things from here on out, I need to be briefed on what's going on. Usually my administrative assistant handles such matters, but she's out on maternity leave and this party is too important to hand off to anyone else."

And what he didn't bother to say because he was certain Dillon had done so already was that this would be the fortieth anniversary of the company his father and uncle had founded. This was not just a special event for the employees, but was important to everyone in the Westmoreland family.

"All right, if you're sure it won't be an inconvenience," she said, breaking into his thoughts.

"It won't be, and I'm on my way."

Alpha Blake tightened her coat around her, feeling totally frustrated. What did a person who had been born in sunny Florida know about the blistering cold of Denver, especially when it had snowed all night and the roads and everything else were covered with white?

But she was so determined to keep her noon appointment with Riley Westmoreland that she'd made a mess of things. Not only would she be late for their appointment, but because of her flat tire they would have to change the location of the meeting and Mr. Westmoreland would be the one driving her there. This was totally embarrassing when she had been trying to make a good impression. Granted, she'd already been hired by Dillon Westmoreland, but when his secretary called last week to say that she would be working with the next man in charge at Blue Ridge, namely Dillon's brother, Riley, she had felt the need to make a good impression on him, as well.

She turned up the heat in her car. Even with a steady stream of hot air coming in through the car vents, she still felt cold, too cold, and wondered if she would ever get used to the Denver weather. Of course it was too late to think about that now. It was her first winter here, and she didn't have any choice but to grin and bear it. When she'd moved, she'd felt that getting as far away from Daytona Beach as she could was essential to her peace of mind, although her friends thought she needed to have her head examined. Who in her right mind would prefer blistering cold Denver to sunny Daytona Beach? Only a person wanting to start a new life and put a painful past behind her.

Her attention was snagged when an SUV pulled off the road to park in front of her. The door swung open and long, denim-clad, boot-wearing legs appeared before a man stepped out of the truck and glanced her way. She met his gaze through the windshield and couldn't help the heart-piercing moment when she literally forgot to breathe. Walking toward her car was a man who was so dangerously masculine, so heart-stoppingly virile, that her brain went momentarily numb.

He was tall, and the Stetson on his head made him appear taller. But his height was secondary to the sharp handsomeness of the features beneath the brim of his hat. There was the coffee-and-cream color of his skin, his piercing dark brown eyes, a perfectly shaped nose, his full lips and a sculpted chin.

And she couldn't bypass his shoulders, massive and powerful-looking. It was hard to believe, with the temperature being what it was, that he seemed comfortable braving the harsh elements with a cowhide jacket instead of a heavy coat. It was in the low teens, and he was walking around like it was in the high sixties.

Her gaze slid all over him as he moved his long limbs toward her vehicle in a walk that was so agile and self-assured, she almost envied the confidence he exuded with every step. Her breasts suddenly peaked, and she could actually feel blood rushing through her veins. She didn't have to guess about what was happening to her, but still, she was surprised. This was the first time she'd reacted to a man since her breakup with Eddie.

The man made it to her car and tapped on the window. She all but held her breath as she pressed the button to roll it down. "Riley Westmoreland?" She really didn't have to ask since he favored his brother, Dillon.

"Yes. Alpha Blake?" he responded, offering her his hand through the open window while looking at her with what she thought was cool and assessing interest.

"Yes." She took his hand and even through her leather gloves, she thought it felt warm. "Glad to meet you, Mr. Westmoreland."

"Riley," he corrected, smiling, and she felt her insides melt. He had a gorgeous pair of eyes. Dark and alluring. "The pleasure is all mine," he added. "I've only heard exceptional things about you and your work. Both Dillon and Pam speak highly of you, Alpha. I hope it's okay for me to call you Alpha."

"Thank you, and yes, that's fine."

"I've made all the arrangements with my road service. Keep your emergency lights on and leave your car keys under your seat," he said, taking a step back so she could get out of the vehicle.

She nervously gnawed her bottom lip. "Will it be safe to do that?"

He chuckled. "Yes, days like this keep thieves inside." He opened the car door for her. "Ready to get inside my truck?"

"Yes." She placed her key under the seat and then grabbed her purse and messenger bag. Tightening her coat around her, she walked quickly to the side of his truck. He was there to open the door and she appreciated finding the inside warm and cozy. It smelled like him, a scent that was masculine and sexy. She blushed, wondering why she was thinking such things, especially about a man she would be working for.

He closed the door just seconds before his cell phone rang, and she looked at the outside mirror as he spoke on the phone while moving around the front of the truck to get in the driver's side.

Opening the door, he climbed inside and proceeded to adjust the seat to accommodate his long legs before snapping his seat belt in place. The call had ended. He put his phone away and glanced over at her with a smile. She thought she would melt right then and there. "Warm?" he asked in a voice that was throatier than anything she'd ever heard.

If only you knew, she fought back saying. Instead her response was a simple "Yes. Thanks for asking."

"No problem." He then glanced into the rearview mirror before easing the truck onto the road.

The ensuing silence gave Riley the impression the woman was shy. And with her wrapped in a bulky coat and standing no more than five foot three, he figured she was probably short and stocky. He preferred tall, slender and curvy, but she had a pretty face that was eye-catching. She was definitely a looker. That had been the first thing he'd noticed. He was a sucker for a pretty face each and every time.

Deciding he didn't like the silence, he reached out and switched on the CD player. Immediately the soulful sound of Jill Scott filled the air. After a few moments, he concluded the music was not enough. To get a dialogue started, he asked conversationally, "I understand you're from Florida. What brought you to Denver?"

She tilted her head to look at him, and the first thing he noticed was her eyes. They were a chocolate brown and oval in shape. Then he was drawn to her hair, a beautiful shade of brown. The thick strands touched her shoulders and curled at the end. The coloring, whether natural or from a bottle, was perfect for her smooth, cocoa-colored complexion. And then there was that cute dimple in her chin, which was there even when she bore a serious expression.

"I've never been the adventurous type, but when my godmother passed away and left me enough funds that I could make a career change without going broke, I took advantage of it."

He nodded. "So what were you doing before you became an event planner?"

"I was a veterinarian."

"Wow. That was some career change."

She smiled. "Yes, it was."

He looked ahead, thinking that if she thought she would not have to explain why someone would stop being a veterinarian to become an event planner, she could think again. "How does a person go from being a vet to becoming a party planner?"

She pushed a lock of hair from her face and said, "Becoming a vet was my parents' idea, and I went along with it."

"Why?" He couldn't imagine going to college for anything other than what he wanted to do in life. He did, however, know how a person could get their dream career waylaid, as in the case of his cousin, Ramsey.

Ramsey had always wanted to be a sheep rancher, and he'd gone to school to study agricultural economics. The only reason Ramsey had taken a CEO position at Blue Ridge Management after school, instead of going into farming, was to work alongside Dillon to keep the company afloat when their parents had died in a plane crash. But once Ramsey and Dillon had made it into a million-dollar company, Ramsey had turned full management of Blue Ridge over to Dillon to become the sheep rancher he'd always wanted to be.

Riley's truck came to a stop at the traffic light, which gave him the opportunity to glance back over at Alpha just in time to see her gnawing her lips again and fidgeting with a sterling silver Tiffany bracelet on her wrist. *Umm, it seems "why" was another uncomfortable question,* he thought.

"I became a vet mainly to satisfy my parents. They own a veterinary clinic and figured I would join them and make it a family affair. I did so for a year, but discovered my heart just wasn't in it. They knew it, but still, they weren't happy when I decided to switch careers. However, they accepted that being an event planner was my calling when I put together their thirtieth wedding anniversary celebration."

"Did a good job of it, huh?" he asked.

She looked over at him and the smile that touched her lips extended from one corner of her mouth to the other and was simply breathtaking. "Yes, I did a bang-up job."

He laughed. "Good for you." He paused a second and asked, "Are you the only child?"

It seemed to take her longer than necessary to answer. "No. I have a sister."

He didn't say anything for a long moment and decided to change the subject. "So what do you have in mind for our employees' holiday bash next month?"

He listened as she went into the details. Some he was able to follow and some he could not. He was a visual person and couldn't use her words to produce mental images. He needed to see actual photographs to get the full effect.

She must have detected such from the expression on his face. "I had prepared a PowerPoint for today. But since we're meeting at the restaurant instead of your office, I—"

"Can still show the presentation. I called ahead and asked for a private meeting room."

"That's great. I have everything I need in here," she said, tapping lightly on the messenger case in her lap.

That caused him to glance down. She was wearing over-the-knee boots, a cute, dark brown leather pair. He glanced back up to her face and saw she was looking out the window, studying the scenery they were passing.

"I never come this way when going to McKay's."

He returned his gaze to the road. "It's a shortcut."

"Oh."

She got quiet again, and this time he decided to let the silence rule. He figured whenever she had anything to say, she would say it. In the meantime, he was perfectly satisfied to sit back and listen to Jill sing her heart out.

Alpha couldn't stop the fluttering in her stomach as she continued to look out the truck's window, trying hard to ignore the man behind the steering wheel. She would have to deal with Riley Westmoreland soon enough when they got to McKay's. She should have known he was drop-dead gorgeous, given Dillon wasn't bad on the eyes. And he seemed to be full of questions. At least he'd already asked two that she wished she could have avoided answering. The reason she had left Daytona was still too painful to think about and after the heated conversation she'd had with her parents last night, she preferred not to think of them right now, either.

Forcing thoughts of Daytona from her mind she saw that they were pulling into the parking lot of McKay's. It seemed the weather was not a deterrent for people wanting to dine at the popular restaurant. The parking lot was full, and Riley had to drive around back to find a spot.

She flexed her hands, liking how the gloves were keeping them warm, and tightened the coat around her as she prepared to get out of the vehicle and confront the cold again. She glanced over at Riley. He wasn't wearing gloves and it seemed the jacket was all he had. She couldn't help asking, "Aren't you cold?"

He smiled over at her. She wished he wouldn't do that because every time he did, he reminded her how long it had been since a man had smiled at her without her questioning his motives.

"Not really. Unlike most, I enjoy cold weather. For me, the colder the better."

She sat there and simply stared at him. He had to be kidding. "Why?"

He shrugged his massive shoulders. "Not sure. I guess I'm too hot-blooded to be bothered."

"Evidently," she said under her breath. If he heard her, he didn't let on. Instead, he opened the door to get out and she released her seat belt and opened her door to do the same. That's when she went sliding and would have fallen flat on her face if Riley hadn't acted quickly to catch her.

"I should have told you to be careful. The ice on the parking lot makes things slippery."

Yes, he should have told her. But if he had, there would have been no reason for his arms to be wrapped around her or for her to be holding on to him for support, feeling the heat of a hot-blooded man so close to her. And that same male scent that had nearly driven her crazy on the ride over wouldn't be doing a number on her.

"I think I can make it now," she said, releasing her tight grip on him.

He kept a firm hand on her arm. "I'll make sure of it." He then swept her off her feet and right into his arms.

Two

Riley entered the restaurant carrying Alpha in his arms. The place was packed with a lunchtime crowd, and Alpha was certain she would die of embarrassment when a number of people watched them.

One man, who was on his way out the door, patted Riley on the back, chuckled and said, "You're still sweeping them off their feet, I see, son."

Riley grinned and replied, "Seems that way, Mr. Daniels." Riley then glanced down at her. "You should be okay from here," he said, putting her on her feet.

"Thanks." She refused to look up at him, but out of the corner of her eye she saw him take a step back. He was probably wishing he was someplace else since she hadn't cost him anything but trouble today.

"Welcome, Riley. The room you requested is ready," the hostess said, smiling, in a way that was a little too friendly, Alpha thought.

"Thanks, I appreciate it, and make sure we aren't disturbed, Paula."

Alpha shouldn't be surprised that the woman knew his name and that he knew hers.

"No problem," Paula said, gesturing for them to follow her. "We gave you the best room in the house." She looked over her shoulder, gave a dismissive glance to Alpha, then looked at Riley directly and said, "Because you deserve the best."

Alpha tried not to frown, wondering if that had been a deliberate dig. Didn't the woman know they were holding a business meeting? So why had she extended her claws?

Alpha felt a thrumming heat in the center of her back when Riley placed his hand there. Even through her coat and all the clothes she had put on to stay warm, she felt his touch and wondered if there would be a permanent handprint on her back.

She blinked when the door closed behind them, and it was then that she glanced around. The room was nice and spacious with a table for two in one corner. There was also a pull-down screen, a projector, speakers and everything else she would need to provide visuals of her plans for the party. And then there was the wall-to-wall window that provided a beautiful view of the mountains. How was anyone expected to work in here with such a gorgeous view?

"Do you want to do it first or eat?"

She swallowed deeply and drew in a deep breath, certain he hadn't meant "it" the way it had sounded. "Whichever you prefer—it's your call."

"In that case, I'll let Paula know we'll eat first. I'm starving."

She nodded, getting distracted watching him slide his jacket off his shoulders. Those massive shoulders were even more broad and powerful than she'd thought. At that moment, she saw firsthand how well his jeans fit his body, especially his tight, masculine thighs, and how they tapered down to his booted feet. He was definitely a hunk if ever there was one, a fine specimen of a man, hands down. He was a sample of pure masculinity, as raw as it could get.

Following his lead, she unbelted her heavy coat and shrugged it off. Then she peeled off her thick, wool sweater, unwrapped the scarf from around her neck and removed another bulky sweater. She had worn as much clothing as she could in order to stay warm.

Walking over to the coatrack to hang up everything she had taken off, she worked the kinks out of her neck and shoulders. Putting on so many garments had weighed her down and stiffened her muscles. She was flipping her hair back off her shoulders when she turned around to find Riley staring at her with an odd expression on his face.

She swallowed, feeling a bit uncomfortable at the way his penetrating dark eyes nearly swallowed her whole. She nervously licked her lips. "Is something wrong?"

Suddenly, a guarded look appeared in his gaze before he glanced out the window. When he switched his gaze back to her the look was gone. "No, nothing's wrong," he said in a brisk tone. "Excuse me for a minute while I let Paula know we'll eat first."

Alpha watched him leave while wondering what that had been all about.

Unnerved to the core, Riley closed the door behind him and leaned against it, releasing a deep breath. Every muscle in his body was thrumming with a need like he hadn't felt in a long time. He was glad the room he'd been given extended off a corridor for privacy…because at that moment he needed it.

Where in the hell had that curvy figure come from? He'd heard of a woman having an hourglass shape, but in all actuality, he'd never truly seen one. Until today.

He couldn't believe what Alpha Blake had been hiding underneath all those clothes. He'd almost dropped his chin to the floor when she started taking off that coat and those sweaters and then stood there in a pink, formfitting sweater dress belted at the waist, with over-the-knee boots. She looked so damn feminine that he'd been jolted with a degree of lust he'd never felt before.

Not only was she a looker, the woman had a body with luscious curves that could make a grown man weep. Lust, as sharp and keen as it could get, was taking over his senses, and the thoughts running through his mind were totally inappropriate, undeniably unacceptable and definitely X-rated.

Her waist was so small that if he blinked he might miss it. And her chest was a perfect size with nice perky breasts. The way the top portion of her dress pressed against those breasts had almost made his eyes pop out of their sockets. And then there was the way her hips flared from her small waist. They were smooth and shapely.

When she had walked over to the coatrack, he had taken it all in. He heard the heel of her boots clicking on the wooden floor and watched with deep male interest how her hips swayed with each step. He was convinced he'd never witnessed anything so sensual. And the shape of her backside filled his mind with all sorts of ideas.

Then she'd turned around and caught him staring. The look in her eyes had been unsettled, and he was sure the look in his had been cautious. That's usually the way it was with him when he'd been caught off guard and had to rebound. He was a man who, under no circumstances, mixed business with pleasure. But he'd wanted that rule to go rolling out the window the moment she'd taken off the coat and those sweaters. Okay, he would admit that it was a physical thing for him, but he couldn't help it. Westmoreland males enjoyed the physical.

"Need help with anything, Riley?"

Paula's question immediately snatched his thoughts back to the present. His gaze roamed up and down the short black hostess outfit she was wearing. Paula Wilmot had a nice body, but even hers couldn't hold a light to Alpha Blake's.

He and Paula had dated a couple of years ago. When it was time for him to move on, she somehow thought some injustice was being done. He had explained up front—as he did with all women he became involved with—that he didn't do long-term flings. Sex with no commitment. One month, six weeks at the most, was all the time he would put into an affair. Not enough time to get sentimental and clingy. That's the way he operated. He called it Riley's rule. Women knew up front what to expect—or not to expect—from him, and he liked it that way.

And the one thing he wouldn't tolerate was someone who agreed to his terms and then decided somewhere along the way to make getting a ring on her finger her number-one goal. All it had taken was a month with Paula to see what her intentions were. For some reason, she'd assumed she would be the woman capable of changing him. It wasn't happening. He'd wasted no time ending things and placing her on his Never Date Again list.

"Yes, please tell our server that my lunch guest and I have decided to eat before getting down to business."

Paula tipped her head to the side as a frown creased her brow. "And I can just imagine what kind of business you intend to get down to, Riley," she said curtly.

His gaze held hers intently. "Can you?"

"Yes. Do I need to remind you that I've been there with you and know just how you operate? So tell me. What does Ms. Frumpy have going for her? Good grief, Riley, I'm sure you can do better."

Frumpy! A vision of the ultrafine body of the woman he'd left in the room floated through his mind. He doubted he could do better. "First of all, this is a business meeting, Paula. Blue Ridge has hired Alpha to handle our holiday party. Secondly, none of my affairs, business or otherwise, are any of your concern." The only reason he'd told her the former was because he knew better than anyone about that vindictive tongue of hers. He refused to have her tarnish Alpha's reputation in any way.

Paula placed her hands on her hips. "One day a woman is going to come along and break your heart. I hope I'm around to see it."

Riley rubbed his hand down his face. Where was all this drama coming from? And why today? Hadn't he woken up in a good mood? "Fine, you've put a curse on me. I guess that means I won't sleep most nights worrying about it," he said, reaching out to open the door.

She quickly reached out and grabbed his hand. "Sorry, Riley, I shouldn't have said that, but you never returned my calls," she said in a frustrated tone.

He stared at her. "No, I haven't, and it's been almost two years, right?"

"Yes."

He nodded slowly, lifting a brow before turning to open the door, hoping she got it that time.

Alpha looked up from her laptop when she heard Riley returning. He glanced around and saw that she had set up the room for the presentation. "I thought we were going to eat first," he said.

"We are. I thought it would save time if I had everything ready so I can move right into my presentation."

He nodded as he sat down at the table. She was about to ask if he could see the huge screen from where he sat when the door opened and a waiter entered, carrying a pitcher of water and menus. Deciding she had wasted Riley's time enough for one day, she moved toward the table when the waiter began filling their glasses with water.

She took the seat across from him and was glad when the waiter handed her a menu. She needed something else, anything else, other than Riley to occupy her attention. She might be wrong, but he seemed upset about something. Was he upset with her?

She placed her menu down. "I'm sorry, Riley."

He glanced up from his own menu and arched a brow. "For what?"

"For getting off to such a bad start with you—having a flat tire, taking you out of your way to come get me, and then having our meeting place changed to accommodate me."

He gave his head a little shake. "No apology necessary. You haven't gotten off to a bad start with me, Alpha. I'm fully aware there are days that don't go quite as well as you'd like. You didn't ask for that flat tire, did you?"

"Goodness, no."

"Then don't worry about it. I'm just glad I was able to help. And as far as having to change our meeting place, McKay's is a favorite of mine, and I'll think of any excuse to get some of their chicken noodle soup. Have you had any?"

She shook her head. "No, I've only eaten their burgers and fries."

He smiled. "Then you don't know what you're missing. You need to try it, if for nothing more than a cup as an appetizer."

He had her curious. "Okay, thanks. I think I will."

She picked up her glass of water to take a sip and then she said, "So you come here often?"

"Yes. Tony McKay and I were good friends all through high school. We went to different colleges and he ended up taking a job in Phoenix. When his father died, he returned to Denver to help his mother close down the restaurant, but decided to stay and run it instead. He wasn't crazy about the job he'd landed after college and his management degree gave him plenty of ideas on how to take this place to a whole new level."

He paused to take another sip of his water. "Old man McKay would not have approved of the changes Tony made, especially with the expansion and keeping the place open until midnight. He didn't believe in change and fought it tooth and nail. Tony and I tried to convince him for years that the only constant was change, and so he might as well get used to it. We told him to embrace it like everyone else so he could stay competitive."

He chuckled. "Tony not only embraces change, but he's implemented a few precedents. Such as convincing our school board to add a culinary class to their high school curriculum and then giving students jobs to gain firsthand experiences while getting class credits."

"Smart move."

Riley smiled. "We thought so."

She glanced back at her menu. "So what else would you suggest other than my usual burger and fries?"

"Umm, you can't go wrong with their chicken. It's covered with the best gravy you can eat and comes with mouthwatering scalloped potatoes and hot buttered yeast rolls."

She couldn't help frowning. "That sounds like a lot of food."

"It is, but if the forecasters are right, you might be snowed in for the next day or two and leftovers would come in handy."

Was that excitement she heard in his voice? "You really do like it, don't you?"

"Like what?"

He glanced over at her, and the moment he did so she felt a zing in the pit of her stomach. Why was her body reacting so much to him? She was twenty-seven and knew all about chemistry between a man and a woman, but she'd never in her life experienced anything so potent. "The cold weather. I thought you were teasing about liking it, but apparently you weren't. Here I was, all bundled up like I was living at the North Pole, and you were wearing a lightweight jacket as if you could barely feel the cold."

He shrugged, and she couldn't help but admire the undulating movement of his shoulders beneath his shirt. "I guess I'm immune. I've been here all my life and was told I was born during one of Denver's worst snowstorms. I've always enjoyed playing in the snow."

He chuckled and the sound floated around the room with such a rich octave it made Alpha draw in a charged breath. "February is my favorite month because that's usually when Denver is the coldest."

Riley leaned back in his chair and her gaze was drawn to his hands. For a quick second, she recalled how those hands had felt when he'd picked her up and carried her into the restaurant. She had felt the warmth of them through the thickness of her clothes.

"Today is nothing compared to how things will get later on," he said, breaking into her thoughts. "Surely you understood what you were doing when you traded sunny Florida for Denver?"

Alpha drew in a deep breath. No, she hadn't fully understood. The only thing she'd known was that she needed to put as much distance between her, Eddie and her parents as she could. "I didn't expect it to be this cold so soon. I figured I would prepare myself for January and February, but it's still November."

"Yes, and Thanksgiving is right around the corner. Are you going back south for turkey and dressing?"

Not on her life. "No. I plan on spending Thanksgiving here since I have a couple of projects during that time." And they were projects she could have gotten out of doing had she wanted to, but she hadn't.

The waiter returned to take their orders, and she was glad for the interruption. She was getting too comfortable with Riley and had to admit that he made such a thing easy. He came across as a nice guy. Down-to-earth. A real gentleman, respectful. It was nice to know that for some men, sex wasn't the only thing on their minds.

Three

Riley shifted in his seat, thinking that if Alpha knew all the things that were going through his mind, she would think he was as low as low could go. He had met her less than two hours ago and all he could think about was jumping her bones. No, jumping her bones was too quick and raunchy. He would love easing between those legs and then…

When he heard the sound of her lightly clearing her throat, he realized the waiter standing beside him had poured cups of coffee and was waiting to take his order. He glanced up at the waiter. George. The seventy-something man had worked at McKay's for ages and had waited on him plenty of times before with many of his other dates. Was that a smirk on George's face because the old man had finally caught him being taken with a woman?

"And what can I get for you, Mr. Westmoreland?"

"The usual, George."

"All right," George said, taking the menu from Riley.

Riley glanced over at Alpha and saw she was absorbed in

the beauty of the mountains that could be seen through the windows. "It's beautiful, isn't it?" he asked, studying her more so than the mountains he'd seen all his life.

"Yes."

Sitting this close to her, he could see just how beautiful, how stunning, she was. That wasn't a good thing. How was he supposed to concentrate on whatever presentation she was giving when he wanted to concentrate on her?

She broke eye contact while reaching for her coffee to take a sip and he did likewise. "So, other than the cold weather, how do you enjoy living in Denver so far?" he asked her.

"I like it. I'm grateful that the people here have been so kind. I didn't expect my business to take off like it has."

"I understand your work speaks for itself. My sister-in-law was definitely impressed."

She smiled. "Pam is super nice."

Their conversation was interrupted when George returned with their appetizers, still wearing that smirk on his face.

Alpha drew in a deep breath. She had done presentations quite a few times and knew there wasn't a shy bone in her body, but standing in front of Riley had butterflies floating around in her stomach.

She looked over at him to find him looking back at her. She forced a smile. "I promise to have you out in fifteen minutes."

"Take your time."

He would say that, she thought. Their waiter had cleared the table and filled their cups.

"The first thing we need to decide on is a theme for that night. These are the ones I came up with while trying to stay away from holiday themes. Because of diversity in the workplace, the last thing you want to do is offend anyone."

"So what do you suggest?" he asked her.

"A winter theme always works. These are a few that I've come up with," she said, clicking the remote in her hand to bring the screen alive. "As you can see, I have Winter Wonderland, Winter Delight, One Winter's Night and Winter Around the World."

She watched him study each suggestion. He shifted his eyes back to her, and she felt her stomach stir from the intensity of his gaze. "What's your favorite?"

"It's really your decision."

He nodded. "I know, but which one do you like the best?"

She glanced up at the screen. "Based on the fact that this year there will be a nighttime party in the ballroom of the Pavilion Hotel, instead of the daytime party you usually hold at the office, I like One Winter's Night. There's a sort of magical ring. I like it."

A smile curved his lips. "So do I. Let's go with it."

Alpha nodded, excited that he'd liked the same theme that she did. "All right. And as far as the ballroom at the Pavilion Hotel, I took a tour a few days ago. It will hold up to two thousand people," she said, showing an aerial view of the huge hotel, which was located midway between downtown and the airport.

"And it's a definite we have it for that night?"

"Yes," she said, smiling. "They were happy to accommodate us. The Westmoreland name carries a lot of weight."

Deciding to move on to the next point, she said, "I thought it would be nice to set the mood by having it be a dressy affair."

He lifted a brow. "How dressy?"

"Black tie." At the grimace on his face, she smiled and quickly said, "Not as bad as all that, Riley. I think your employees will appreciate it. It will make them feel special. Other than your family's annual charity ball, your employees probably never have anyplace to go where they can dress up and feel as if they're stepping out on the town."

He nodded slowly, and she knew he was thinking about the idea. She just wished she didn't feel that sexual chemistry between them even while discussing business. "Let's table that for at least a week," he suggested.

"All right," she said. "But I'll need a decision on the attire in order to determine what sort of decorations will be appropriate."

"I'll keep that in mind."

"Last but not least," she said, switching off the screen, "is the discussion of the budget. That handout I've given you breaks everything down. I inflated the expenses to allow for decorations. I'd rather operate on the high end versus a low one."

She paused a moment and then said, "Those are all of my ideas and suggestions. Is there anything you want to add or change?"

He shook his head. "No, I think you did a thorough job explaining things."

"Thank you," she said, crossing the room to place the remote near the television screen. That's when she dropped her ink pen and leaned down to pick it up.

For the second time that day Riley was slapped with a case of lust so thick he wondered how in the hell he was going to stand without giving away his body's reaction. She had leaned down to pick up her pen, and the way the material of her dress stretched snug across that gorgeous backside, he'd almost swallowed his tongue. Drawing in a deep breath, he used his hand to wipe away the perspiration forming on his forehead.

"Need help with anything?"

"No, thanks," she said, flicking a quick glance in his direction before returning to what she was doing. He continued to sit there, almost willing her to glance back at him, hold his gaze, feel his heat and not deny the potent chemistry flowing between them.

At that moment, he made a decision. "We'll need to meet

again next week, after I've reached a decision about the attire for the event."

He knew she was probably wondering why they needed to meet to discuss that when it was something they could cover over the phone. Instead of questioning him about anything, though, she simply said, "That's fine. Do you know when and where?"

"I'll call you."

She met his gaze and held it. He knew at that moment that if she hadn't felt the strong undercurrents flowing between them before, she did now. "All right."

Now that was where he disagreed with her. It wasn't all right, but he didn't know a way to change the path he seemed determined to take where she was concerned.

He watched as she re-dressed in her two heavy sweaters, scarf, huge overcoat and gloves. Was all that necessary? Evidently to her they were. If she wanted to stay warm the best thing she needed was body heat. Namely, his.

"I'm ready to go."

Glad he had gotten his body under control and that there was no sign of the lust that had overtaken it earlier, he stood. "Do I need to carry you out?" he teased.

Her eyes rounded and it amused him that she'd assumed he was serious. "No, and I'm sorry you felt the need to do so before. I'm usually not clumsy," she said apologetically.

"You weren't clumsy, Alpha. You aren't used to walking on icy, slippery surfaces and that's understandable. Will you do me a favor?"

She tilted up her head to look at him. "What?"

"Stop apologizing. You haven't done anything wrong."

"Thanks."

"Doing that must drive your boyfriend crazy," he said, deliberately fishing for information.

"I don't have a boyfriend."

"Oh." He placed his hand in the center of her back as he led her out of the room. So she didn't have a boyfriend. Hmm.

An hour or so later Alpha entered her home and immediately shrugged off her heavy coat and began peeling off her sweaters and gloves. It was then that she missed her scarf and figured she must have left it in Riley's truck.

During their ride back to her car she'd noticed he no longer seemed to be on guard with her, the way he had been at the restaurant earlier, and she took advantage by keeping the conversation going about the holiday party—One Winter's Night. The more she talked about it the more excited she got.

Once they reached her car, she saw her tire was fixed and her car keys were back where she'd left them. He wouldn't accept any money for having her tire taken care of, so she thanked him for lunch. After assuring him she would follow up with him in a week to discuss the attire for the party, she hurried off to her car. He had sat in his truck, watching her drive off.

Now she was home, inside the house she'd fallen in love with the first time she'd seen it. The last house in the cul-de-sac of a street where all the backyards faced the mountains, it was smaller than her place in Daytona but she'd always thought her condo on the beach had been too large for her anyway. Now she didn't have any wasted space, and the windows facing her backyard provided a gorgeous view of the mountains. However, there were days she missed the beach, until she remembered she had given up the beach for a reason.

Sitting down on the sofa, she began removing her boots. The first thing she'd done after buying the house was carpet the majority of the tile floors. The thought of getting out of bed and letting her feet touch cold tile had sent chills up her body. Other than that she hadn't changed a thing. Definitely not the extensive woodwork trim or the custom cabinets.

Moments later, taking her shoes in her hand, she walked

in bare feet to her bedroom while thinking about what had driven her here to Denver.

Eddie Swisher.

At one time, she had thought he was everything she had wanted in a man. In the end, she'd discovered he was nothing more than a puppet with his parents pulling the strings. She would never forget the day, a mere week before her wedding, when he had shown up at her place and dropped the bomb. A family meeting had been called and his family had voted. It had been decided that he couldn't marry her unless she vowed to disown Omega, her twin sister—the former porn star. After all, he had pointed out, her own parents had turned their backs on Omega. He couldn't understand why she wouldn't do the same. It had meant nothing to him that Omega was no longer in the business or that she had met a man who'd adored her regardless of her past. It was a past her parents and Eddie just couldn't get beyond.

At least he hadn't stooped to the same level as LeBron Roberts, the guy she'd dated before Eddie. When LeBron had learned of her twin's occupation, he'd assumed Alpha would miraculously transform into Omega in the bedroom. When she had dashed those hopes, he hadn't wasted any time in dropping her.

Her thoughts shifted back to Riley. He was a fine specimen of a man, definitely a threat to the peace she was trying to find. It didn't take much for her to remember those beautiful dark eyes, long lashes and the way his jaw curved whenever he smiled. She'd never been drawn to any male with such intensity. He took the word *sexy* to all new heights. She had been attracted to LeBron and Eddie but not to the same degree. It was something about his voice, the way he looked at her, his entire presence that made her think of long winter nights—with him.

She tossed the hair from her face, thinking she had truly gotten her drool-on today, whether he knew it or not. And it was best that he didn't know since it couldn't lead anywhere. She had definitely learned her lesson. When her relationship with Eddie ended she had vowed not to get seriously involved with another man. It wasn't worth the pain and hassle.

She dropped her boots in the closet and, leaving her bedroom, moved on to her family room. It was small and cozy. At the moment, she wanted cozy. She would curl up on her sofa and find something interesting on television. Or better yet, she could just relive her time with Riley. For just a little while, she would wallow in fantasies and then, later, she would get up and try getting some work done.

Riley sat on the sofa in his living room in front of his fireplace, drinking a cold beer while replaying in his mind his encounter with Alpha. Now that he had satisfied his curiosity about her, knew she was competent and could handle what Dillon had hired her to do, he could easily delegate any one of his supervisors to work with her. But he didn't want to do that, and for the life of him he couldn't understand why, especially when it was obvious the woman posed a lot of problems for him.

He knew that she had the ability to drive any man to distraction, which was the last thing he needed. No other woman had been capable of doing such a thing to him, but after meeting her today, he believed that she could, physically and mentally. The thought that he was even considering mixing business with pleasure was the first sign that he had messed up somewhere. He'd allowed her to get under his skin. But with single-minded determination, he intended to get her out.

He had learned his lesson by watching how obsessed his youngest brother, Bane, had been with Crystal Newsome and the heartbreak Bane had suffered when the teenage lovers had been forced apart.

Riley released a deep sigh. Bane had been the last child born to his parents, and everyone had assumed Bane would be a girl, the daughter their parents didn't have. Things didn't turn out that way. They'd gotten Bane. Personally, Riley had been happy about it. Who wanted a sister anyway? He had his girl cousins, Megan and Gemma, and as far as he was concerned, they were enough. So he'd become Bane's protector while growing up, or at least he'd tried. But he hadn't been able to foresee the pain Bane would suffer when, at eighteen, he fell in love with sixteen-year-old Crystal. Her parents had been against the match from the start and had separated the teens by sending Crystal away to parts unknown.

Riley would never forget that day for as long as he lived. A heartbroken Bane had ridden his horse out alone. When he hadn't returned at a reasonable hour, Dillon had gotten worried and sent Riley looking for him.

He had found Bane in an old abandoned shack that had been on the Westmoreland property for years. The moment Riley had entered the place he'd known it had been Crystal and Bane's love nest. But what had really gripped Riley's insides was the sound of Bane howling like a tormented and wounded animal.

Riley had actually felt his brother's pain and heartbreak that day. The sound had pierced something deep within him, and he'd wondered what there was about love that could torture and torment even a badass dude like Bane. On that day he'd vowed never to find out.

Without letting Bane know he was there, Riley had backed out of the shack and left, allowing his brother to grieve privately for the love he'd lost. That had been several years ago, but Riley's vow to never fall for a woman hadn't changed. That's when he had implemented Riley's Rule.

Reaching out, he picked up the wool scarf Alpha had left in his truck and brought it to his nose. It smelled like her. Sweet. Womanly. Enticing…so damn enticing. And the scent reminded him of all the heated desire that had warped his senses during the time he'd been with her. It was heated desire that was still slowly driving him insane.

He placed the scarf aside and picked up his cell phone to redial the number that had come through that morning. He felt his stomach tighten when he heard her soft voice.

"Hello?"

"Alpha? This is Riley. You left your scarf in my truck, and I want to get it back to you. Will you be home tomorrow?"

There was a slight hesitation and then she said, "Yes, but you don't have to come out of your way to return it, Riley. I have several of them."

"No problem. I want to make sure you get this one back. You live in the Arlington Heights area, right?"

"Yes."

"I'll be out that way tomorrow around two. Is it okay for me to drop by?"

Another slight hesitation. "Yes, I'll be home."

"Fine, I'll see you then."

Riley clicked off the phone. He was doing the decent thing by returning the scarf and nothing more. The thought that he was itching to see her again had nothing to do with it.

He brought the scarf to his nose once more. Yes, he definitely wanted to see her again.

Four

"I should have been more forceful about him not returning that darn scarf," Alpha muttered as she glanced at herself again in the full-length mirror in her bedroom. "I guess, considering the layers of clothes I was wearing to keep warm yesterday, he figured I must need every piece."

Drawing in a deep breath, she licked her lips, wondering if she should put on lipstick. If she did, he might assume she'd gotten pretty just for him. She frowned, knowing that, in essence, she had. Wednesday was the day she usually did housework and seldom put anything on other than her sweats. But not today.

She had awakened and quickly straightened up, eaten lunch, baked her favorite cinnamon rolls, showered and dressed in a canary-yellow buttoned shirt that tied at the waist and a denim skirt that hit above the knee. A pair of striped, black-and-white ballet flats that she had purchased before leaving Daytona were on her feet.

"I look cute, if I have to say so myself," she said softly and then threw her head back and laughed. When was the last time she had gone to a lot of trouble to look good for a man? Why was she doing so now?

Okay, she thought, deciding to put on lipstick after all, she would answer the first question. The last time had been for her parents' anniversary party a year or so ago and the man had been Eddie. In all honesty, she had stopped thinking of her and Eddie as a couple long before he'd given her that ultimatum about Omega. They had begun drifting apart. Once she had gotten serious about becoming an event planner they had found excuse after excuse to not spend time together. It hadn't bothered her, and she had a feeling it hadn't bothered him, either. Yet neither of them had made a move to call off their wedding for those reasons.

Her thoughts drifted back to the second half of the question she'd asked herself. Why was she going out of her way to look good for Riley? It could be that a part of her wanted to feel like a woman—a woman any man could be interested in, a woman a man could and would notice.

He *had* noticed the other day, which surprised her when she'd caught him staring. She hadn't expected him to display as strong a reaction to her as she had to him. And she was certain she hadn't imagined it. It had been there in his eyes when she'd turned around. Although it had been quickly replaced with a guarded look, it had been there.

"Okay, for the first time in a long time I feel like a desirable woman, and I like it," she said, after applying her lipstick and pursing her lips to see the effect.

Even before they'd broken up, Eddie had stopped going out of his way to make her feel like she could rock his world. But with Riley the sparks had been there, and they were sparks that sizzled. They had both tried to downplay it, but hadn't been successful. And that was one of the things that concerned her. Would the sparks be there when she saw him again today?

She was about to take the comb and work with her hair some more when she heard the doorbell. Riley was early. A good five minutes early. Looking at herself in the mirror one last time, she tied her hair back from her face before quickly leaving her bedroom. She headed for the door, not sure if those five minutes were a good thing or a bad thing.

Riley glanced around. Nice house. The stucco structure with an A-line roof and carved columns on the porch suited her. The Arlington Heights area was one of the oldest in Denver, but he could tell her home had been added within the past ten years or so. She had a pretty nice neighborhood. Quiet. Serene. Mountains as a backdrop and snow-covered yard. It had snowed again overnight and was slow in melting.

On the drive over, he kept asking himself what he was doing. He could easily mail the scarf to her, return it when they met again next week or keep it for a souvenir. But here he was, standing on her doorstep like a lust-craved addict eager for one glimpse of her.

Okay, who was he kidding? He wanted more than a glimpse. He wanted *her*. In his bed. There was no reason for him to deny it because it was true. He had tried talking himself out of wanting her all through the night but had failed miserably. In the end, he'd figured that as long as he applied Riley's Rule he would be safe. And as for mixing business with pleasure, technically, she was on contract and not a real employee of Blue Ridge. Now, if he could get her to go along with his proposition, then an affair would be a surefire way of taking care of this desire before she had a chance to get deeper into his system.

He heard her at the door and knew she had looked out the peephole at him. He had felt her checking him out, which was fine since he planned on checking her out, as well. Chances were she wasn't covered in all those coats and sweaters today. Hell, he hoped not.

The door opened, and she stood there. He had to clamp his jaws together to stop them from dropping. If he'd thought she looked good yesterday then he was totally unprepared for how stunning she looked today. His gaze roamed over her, and he quickly decided that he loved her outfit. It emphasized her figure.

"Riley."

"Alpha."

She licked her lips, and his stomach tightened. Not for the first time, he thought she had a nice-looking tongue. He couldn't wait to taste it.

"You brought the scarf?" she asked, intruding into his thoughts.

"Yes." Did she expect him to hand it over to her right here and now and then leave? Did she not expect him to hang around for a few minutes? He hadn't thought of that possibility.

He pulled the scarf out of his jacket pocket. "Here's the scarf."

She took it. "Thanks." And then she asked the question he'd been waiting for, the one he had begun to fear she wouldn't ask. "Would you like to come in? I just made a fresh pot of coffee and was about to have a cup with some cinnamon rolls I made earlier."

He forced his feet to stay put and not rush past her. "Sounds good. Yes, I'd like a cup of coffee and rolls."

She moved aside and he walked in, inhaling her scent as he brushed by her. It was the same scent on the scarf. He glanced around her home, admiring the furnishings, crown moldings, spindle staircase and beautiful light fixtures in the ceiling. She had a great room with a huge fireplace, and he loved that a blaze was going inside of it, throwing warmth into the room.

"Would you like to give me your jacket?"

He glanced over at her. "Sure," he said, shrugging off his

jacket and handing it to her. She walked over to the coatrack, and he watched her every move. He had to clamp down on his lips to not let out a whistle. The woman had the most gorgeous legs he'd ever seen. When she turned around, there was no need to act innocent. He'd been caught red-handed checking out her legs.

He cleared his throat. "Nice shoes."

"Thanks."

"Different." Although he hadn't been concentrating on her shoes, they *were* different. Striped.

She glanced down at them. "Different but comfortable. Do you want your coffee out here or in the kitchen?"

He shoved his hands inside the pockets of his jeans. "Where do you usually take yours?"

"In the kitchen."

"Then lead the way."

And she did. He deliberately stayed a few paces behind her to check out her legs, waist and backside. And no, he had no shame. She had more sensuality in her walk than some women had in their entire bodies, and the male in him felt the need to take the time to appreciate it.

She was wearing flats, but with her shapely calves he could just imagine those legs in a pair of stilettos. Her skirt was a decent length, but if it had been just a tad shorter he would probably have already had a heart attack. At that moment, he felt blood rushing straight to his groin.

He walked into her kitchen and stopped, equally impressed by the custom maple cabinets, granite countertops and stainless-steel appliances. The high-top café table was facing a huge window overlooking her backyard, which included a view of the mountains.

"How do you take your coffee?"

He glanced over at her. "Black and as strong as you can get it."

She smiled. "My dad drinks his the same way."

"Does he?" he asked, sliding onto a bar stool.

"Yes. My mom prefers hot chocolate and so did I."

She brought the coffee to him with a tray of sweet-smelling rolls. They looked fresh, hot and delicious. Just like her. He took a sip of coffee. It was good, just like he figured she would be. He bit into a roll and closed his eyes. It was delicious.

He opened his eyes and found her smiling at him. "Hit a sweet tooth, huh?" she asked.

If only she knew. "Homemade?"

"Yes, one of my mom's old recipes. She likes to bake."

"It's delicious," he said, taking another bite and then gobbling up the rest of it while thinking he would love gobbling her up in the same way.

"You can have another. I ate a couple earlier."

"Thanks." He didn't waste time taking her up on her offer, grabbing another one off the plate and biting into it.

"Thanks for bringing my scarf back, but like I told you, you didn't have to do it. It could have waited."

Riley glanced over at her, thinking that, no, it could not have waited. He was one of those men who, once he made up his mind about something, there was no turning back, no hesitation and no stopping him. He hadn't been in an affair for about four months now, mainly because he'd had a lot on his plate at the office while taking over for Dillon. Now that he had things at a level where he could work without too much stress, he had time for some of the finer, more enjoyable things in life. All work and no play wasn't good for anyone.

"The reason I brought the scarf back, Alpha, is because I wanted to see you again. And I would have found any excuse to do so."

He watched her expression. She probably hadn't counted on him being so in-your-face honest. But he always was at the beginning of his affairs...and at the end.

She licked her lips. He was beginning to recognize that as a sign that she was nervous. She held his gaze for a moment and asked after taking a sip of coffee, "Would you have... found any excuse?"

"Yes. We're adults, and I don't like playing games. I believe in being up-front with any woman I'm interested in."

"And you're interested in me?"

He heard the surprise in her voice. "Yes, but you should have known that after yesterday. There is chemistry between us. A lot of it. I could barely watch you while you gave that presentation without getting turned on."

Maybe he'd given her too much information, but he wanted her to know just what he was dealing with. What they were both dealing with, because although she hadn't admitted anything yet, he had a gut feeling she was as attracted to him as he was to her.

She looked down and nervously began toying with her paper napkin, but he preferred that she look at him. He needed to know what she was thinking. "Alpha?"

She glanced up, and the look he saw in her eyes made his stomach quiver all the way to his groin. That same potent chemistry, that electrical sizzle, they had shared yesterday was present today whether she wanted it to be or not. It was just as strong and powerful...but he could tell she was fighting it tooth and nail. Why?

"We just met yesterday," she said softly.

He nodded. She had to do better than that. As far as he was concerned meeting just yesterday didn't mean a thing. People were into one-night stands. He'd done a number of those himself. "And?"

"And I'm working for you."

Okay, now she was trying to play the "it's not ethical" card, but it wouldn't work. "No, you're not working for me, at least you're not my employee. You're on assignment for Blue Ridge Land Management for a project that ends next month. As far as I'm concerned that has nothing to do with what's going on between us."

"There's nothing going on between us," she said, taking another sip of coffee.

Now she wanted to be in denial and he wasn't going along with that, either. He leaned back in his chair and stared at her. For a long moment he didn't say anything and then he said, "I want to know why you're sitting there denying what is so blatantly obvious."

Her lips began quivering, in anger or desire he wasn't sure, but neither curtailed the electricity sizzling between them. "And just what do you think is so blatantly obvious?" she asked in a quiet tone.

He reached out and placed his hand over hers. The moment he did so, he felt what she wanted to deny. A heated spiral of desire flowed between them, and she gasped softly. He wanted her to feel it. He needed her to feel it. And he knew by the look in her eyes that she had.

"What is so blatantly obvious, Alpha, is that I want you and you want me."

Alpha couldn't stop the chaotic fluttering in her stomach. Nor could she slow down the beating of her heart. What was Riley doing to her? What was he making her feel? All these incredible sensations that she'd never felt before were swamping her all at once.

She tried to force herself to think logically. She needed to make him understand something about her. "I've never been a woman to engage in casual relationships, Riley."

"There's a first time for everything, isn't there?" he asked, still holding her gaze as if he was looking deep into her very soul.

Yes, there was a first time for everything, but she wasn't sure she was ready for what she knew would be nothing more than a fling. But another part of her was demanding to know *why* she wasn't ready. She had moved from Florida to Colorado to start a new life. It wasn't that she hadn't gotten over

Eddie, because she had. So what was the holdup? Riley was ultrahandsome, much too sexy, and he was attracted to her. Why was she afraid to go with the flow?

He leaned in close to her. "In that case, I propose we take some time to get to know each other, but…"

She'd known there was going to be a *but* in there somewhere.

"But that we enjoy each other while doing so."

Her pulse quickened. She didn't have to ask how they would enjoy each other. The man was pushing all her buttons, in ways she hadn't known existed. He was making her consider doing things she'd never thought of doing before.

"With all of my affairs there are rules so we have a good understanding from day one," he added.

She lifted an arched brow. "What rules?"

He smiled. "First, there needs to be a time limit on how long the affair will last. Definitely no longer than six weeks."

She nodded. "What else?"

"There has to be exclusivity. I'm not into sharing. Neither am I into clinginess. This affair doesn't give us the right to crowd each other. We need to respect each other's space."

Evidently he'd had issues in the past. Well, he wouldn't have to worry about those issues with her. "Okay."

"And if, for whatever reason, the rules are broken by either of us, the affair ends," he said.

His rules were reasonable, but still… "I need to think about it," she said. At least he was being honest by letting her know up front what he wanted out of a relationship. She could appreciate that.

"That's fine. Since we need to meet next week to discuss some things regarding the party, you can give me your answer then. What about Monday? Hopefully the weather will be better and we can meet at my office. Let's say around ten. Is that time okay for you?"

"Yes, ten o'clock will work."

"Good." He stood. "I'm sure you have a lot to do today, so I'll be going. Thanks for the coffee and rolls."

She stood as well, thinking how his height seemed to dominate the room. She never thought her kitchen was small until now. "You're welcome."

He took her hand and held it gently in his while they walked through her great room back toward the door. Hand-holding was something she'd always craved but something Eddie had never delivered. He wasn't a touchy-feely type.

When they reached the door she turned to Riley, to again thank him for returning her scarf, but the words died on her lips. He had the most irresistible smile, one that showed his dimples. To distract herself, she looked over his shoulder at the picture hanging on her wall, but Riley lifted his hand to cup her chin and return her gaze to him. Then he softly trailed his fingertips along the lines of her jaw.

In that heated moment, when their eyes connected, she felt a sensual connection to him all the way to her toes. She wanted to take a step back but couldn't. Like he'd said, she couldn't deny what was taking place between them.

"I want to leave you with something to think about."

She didn't have to ask what that something was because she knew. The rippling of coiled anticipation in her stomach spelled it out for her. He was about to stamp his presence all over her, and she would do more than think about it, she would fantasize about it for years to come.

Her heart skipped a few beats when he released her chin to ease his arms around her waist and settle his hands right above her backside. Then he took a step closer while their gazes remained connected. There was a heated resolve in the dark depths of the eyes staring into hers. And when she saw him lowering his head, her feet—of their own accord—arched on tiptoes so she could meet his lips. All those amazing and incredible feelings she'd encountered since meeting him totally obliterated her senses.

The man had all but admitted the only thing he wanted from her was sex, but she hadn't decided whether or not he would be getting what he wanted. All she cared about for the time being was locking her lips with his, taking in more of his scent and acquiring his taste. She was tired of dealing with all these crazy emotions and sensations. She wanted relief, and she knew one place where she could find it.

Right here, she thought, the moment Riley's mouth aimed straight for hers.

His tongue entered her on impact, and she responded on instinct. Reaching up, she wrapped her arms around his neck and pressed her body closer to his. No kiss had ever made her feel like this. Riley was a master at using his tongue, and he was doing so with a skill that nearly brought her to her knees. He explored first one side of her mouth then the other. And he was doing it with such intimacy that she felt it deep in her bones.

He was taking her mouth greedily, as if this was his one-and-only chance. He was giving a whole new definition to French-kissing, and she moaned with every lick, every suck and every blatant stroke.

Alpha was certain she would lose her mind if Riley didn't let go of her mouth, and he seemed in no hurry to release it. Instead, he continued to take it in an even deeper kiss, stroking his tongue in a way that sent high degrees of desire spreading all through her. The hard bluntness of his arousal pressed like steel into her belly, and she moved her body to cradle it in the juncture of her thighs.

She knew he was intentionally driving her mad, branding her and leaving his mark. The heat flaring in her midsection was sending her hormones—which were getting his name stamped all over them—raging out of control.

And then he slowly pulled his mouth away. Heavy-lidded dark eyes remained steady on her. She tried to stop the way her stomach was quivering and found she wasn't able to do so. Nothing was capable of bringing a halt to the sensations stampeding through her.

"Now, a promise to you, Alpha. If you agree to what I suggested," he said in a low, throaty voice, "I'll make sure that we enjoy each other in a way no two humans have ever done."

He then leaned down and lightly brushed the tip of his tongue across her lips before opening the door and walking out of it.

Five

Riley thought this had been the longest week of his life. Now the day had finally arrived when he would be seeing Alpha again. More than once he'd been tempted to come up with any excuse to pick up the phone and call her to see how she was coming along in her thought processes regarding the affair he'd proposed.

He would find out in a couple of hours at their scheduled meeting. He'd even arrived to work early, had advised the receptionist covering the lobby to send Alpha in as soon as she arrived. There was no need for her to wait. He was tired of waiting.

There was a knock on his door, and he knew from the three repetitive knuckle raps that it was his brother, Canyon. Dropping by Riley's office at the start of the workday was the norm for both Canyon and his other brother, Stern. Riley was eleven months older than Canyon and almost two years older than Stern. The three of them had been close while growing up, and although they didn't always agree on everything, they had deep respect for one another. Working for the family firm after college had always been their goal in life, and they enjoyed working alongside Dillon to preserve the legacy their father and uncle had begun. All his brothers worked in some capacity at Blue Ridge except for Micah, who was an epidemiologist with the federal government; Jason, who, along with cousins Zane and Derringer, was in the horse training and breeding business; and Riley's youngest brother, Bane, who was in the navy.

"Come in."

Canyon, who was one of the firm's attorneys, quickly walked in with his briefcase in hand. "I need to run something by you, Ry. It's that dispute we're trying to settle out of court with Shade Tree Developers. We're holding our initial meeting tomorrow."

Riley looked at his watch. "Okay, I have less than a half hour to spare, so make it quick."

Canyon lifted a brow. "And just what fire are you going to?"

Riley tossed aside some papers on his desk. "No fire, just an important meeting at ten."

"With who?"

If Riley didn't know of his brother's penchant for being inquisitive, he would have been annoyed with Canyon's questions. "I'm meeting with our event planner, Alpha Blake, about the holiday party next month."

"Oh," Canyon said with a smirk on his face. He took the chair in front of Riley's desk. Riley knew why the smirk was there. Dillon had tossed the responsibility to both of them and neither had wanted it. In the end, they'd drawn straws. Riley hadn't been happy that he'd been the one to lose, but now he was more than glad that he had.

"Okay, Canyon, what's going on with Shade Tree Developers?" he asked, deciding to steer his brother away from the subject of Alpha.

"I talked with one of their new attorneys today. She was brought on board a couple of weeks ago and you won't believe who she is."

"Who?"

"Keisha Ashford."

Riley scrunched up his face, remembering. "Is that the same Keisha you had that affair with a few years ago?"

Canyon shifted in his seat. "One and the same."

"Ouch." Riley remembered the affair hadn't ended well.

"Yes, that's what I said. However, she sounded pleasant enough."

Riley chuckled and leaned back in his chair with his arms raised and resting against the back of his neck. "They always do, even when they're about to cut off your balls. I told you to always be up-front with a woman. You set the parameters and the rules. Then there'll be less drama on the back end. That's why I have Riley's Rules. That's the only way I operate."

While Canyon rambled on with nonsense about not all women agreeing to rules, Riley's thoughts shifted back to Alpha. He had already spelled out his terms and she could take them or leave them.

He was hoping like hell that she took them.

Alpha stepped off the elevator onto the fortieth floor of the Blue Ridge Management building where the executive offices were located. She recalled the first time she'd come here, last month, to meet with Dillon and how impressed she'd been with the plush surroundings the moment she'd walked inside the building.

First, there had been the huge, beautifully decorated atrium with a waterfall amidst a replica of mountains, complete with blooming flowers and other foliage. Seeing all those flowers had reminded her of a spring day in Daytona when flowers sprouted everywhere. They were the first sign that the city should prepare for spring break, when all the college students would hit the beaches.

She liked the feel of the thick, luxurious carpet beneath her shoes. The first thing that caught her eye today, just like the last time, were the huge portraits of two couples that hung on the main wall in the lobby. They were Riley's parents and his aunt and uncle, who'd all perished in an airplane accident. Four beautiful people who had died young and left behind offspring who loved them. And speaking of love, the photographer who'd taken the photographs had captured the essence of love in both portraits. The way the two women were leaning in toward their husbands, the smiles they wore and the way the couples held hands showed that they'd truly loved each other. She would like to think that seeing these photographs gave the Westmorelands the strength to go on when others would have given up. She couldn't help but admire the way they had bonded together in a crisis, a response which had been so unlike her own family's.

She glanced at her watch and saw she was ten minutes early. The weather was a lot better than last week now that the snowstorm had passed. However, she knew that it was just the beginning and forecasters had already predicted a lot of cold weather ahead.

Alpha tried ignoring the stirring in the pit of her stomach when she approached a bank of offices. She drew in a deep breath when she reached the one with Riley's name elegantly carved in bold gold script. She had no reason to be nervous since he had given her enough time to make a decision and she had. It was one she would live with and not regret making.

She would have an affair with him because, whether she understood why or not, she wanted him. It was as if he had cast some spell on her and even when she'd tried talking herself out of wanting him, she couldn't. So against her better judgment, she would follow the cravings of her body. For once in her life, she would give in to her wants. Besides, after

Eddie had told her he wouldn't marry her, she had pretty much known she wouldn't set herself up for that kind of heartbreak again. A serious relationship with any man was totally out of the question. And she was curious about all that pleasure Riley had talked about.

Another thing she had taken into consideration was that she knew, at some point, she would date again. Although she was certain there were a lot of single men in Denver, she wasn't sure just how decent they were. She considered Riley both decent and honest. He'd demonstrated that by being up-front with her. He hadn't tried sugarcoating an affair or making it out to be more than what it would be. He wanted her. In his bed. Just like she wanted him in hers. No excuses. Just bald facts.

She let out another deep breath. Thinking that way was one thing but actually doing it was another. Growing up, Omega would tease her about talking a good talk, but when the time came to back it up, that was another story. Alpha hoped to do things differently this time around.

She opened the door to another elegant-looking lobby. A young woman sat at the receptionist desk and smiled when she walked in. "Ms. Blake?"

Alpha was surprised the woman knew who she was. "Yes?"

"Mr. Westmoreland has been waiting for you."

Alpha lifted a brow before glancing down at her watch. "But I'm not late."

The young woman chuckled. "Yes, I know, but he's checked three times to see if you've arrived, although I assured him that I would send you in the moment you got here. I guess this meeting is pretty important." The woman then picked up the phone and announced her arrival to Riley.

No sooner had the last word left the woman's lips than Riley's office door was snatched open and he stood there. This was the first time she had seen him in business attire. The transformation left her speechless. He was dressed in a gray suit and a white shirt. The printed tie brought both together and all three complemented the brown coloring of his skin. The cut of his suit did everything to emphasize his masculine build. He looked so handsome standing there, dominating the doorway in such a way that she had to force her breathing to slow. But she could do nothing about the way her blood was rushing through her veins.

The corners of his mouth curved in a heart-stopping smile. "Ms. Blake."

She released the breath she hadn't known she was holding. "Mr. Westmoreland. I have all the information we discussed last week," she said with professional decorum, for the benefit of their audience of one.

He nodded. "Good, I'm anxious for us to get started since we have a lot to cover." He averted his gaze from her to the woman sitting at the desk, who was watching them with interest. "Make sure we're not disturbed until our meeting is over."

"Yes, sir."

He then shifted his glance back to Alpha and stepped aside. "Ms. Blake, please come in."

The thoughts running through Riley's mind when Alpha passed him by were too dangerous to think about at the moment. Why did she always have to smell so darn good? Fresh, sweet and all woman.

She moved to stand in front of his desk and turned around. He remained standing with his back against the closed door with his hands shoved into his pockets. He studied her, thinking every single thing about her spelled *SENSUOUS* in capital letters.

"I've researched more information on the party and have a proposed budget for—"

"You look nice, Alpha," he interrupted her spiel to say. When she began nibbling on her bottom lip, he knew that he was making her nervous but he couldn't help it. He was obsessed, and at that moment he offered no excuses for being so. There was just something about seeing a woman in a business suit with pumps on her feet. Had she assumed her attire would make him want to get down to real business, without thoughts of making love to her? If so, the intent failed miserably.

"Thank you. Now can we get down to—"

"Business?" He gave a negative shake of his head said. "No, not yet."

He slid his hands from his pockets. She was right; they should get down to business. He could go even further and say there was really no reason they should be meeting today at all. The information she was here to give him regarding the party could have been done over the phone. He knew that and figured she knew that, as well.

"What have you decided?" he asked, tempted to walk over to her but knowing if he did he wouldn't be able to keep his hands to himself.

She averted her gaze momentarily and when she looked back, she said, "Maybe we ought to discuss this at another—"

"Alpha."

The menacing tone of his voice probably pretty much told her she could forget that suggestion. "All right, then," she said, placing her messenger bag on his desk. She then glanced over at him. "You were right about there being this strong attraction between us. I've thought about it and considered all aspects of what you've suggested, although, like I told you, I've never engaged in a casual affair—sex with no commitments—before."

"But you've reached a decision?" he asked, noting her expression wasn't giving anything away.

"Yes."

Both hope and despair flooded his stomach at the same time since he had no idea what her decision was. He said nothing, just waited for her to go on. When she didn't, he asked simply, "And?"

She nervously licked her lips again before lifting her chin. "I agree to it, but I have a few rules of my own."

That surprised him. No other woman ever had. He moved from the door to stand beside his desk. "Do you?"

"Yes. First of all, I don't want us to rush into anything."

"You mean not rush into sharing a bed?" he asked for clarity.

"Yes. Like I told you, I'm not used to engaging in casual affairs so it's not anything I can just jump into. I'm going to need time to get used to this."

He wondered how much time she would need. The affair was only supposed to last six weeks at the max. But then the last thing he wanted was a reluctant woman in his bed. Besides, there were ways of breaking down her defenses. "I can agree with that."

She nodded. "And another thing."

"Yes?"

She paused, as if she needed the courage to say her next words. "It's about that promise you made last week, right before leaving my house."

He knew what promise she was referring to and remembered it well. "What about it?"

"I'm holding you to it."

Riley said nothing. He only stared at her. But he wasn't *just* staring at her, Alpha thought. He was doing so in a way that was tantalizing her senses and sending electrified sensations all through her pores. Omega would never believe Alpha was letting any man affect her this way. Or that she was drawn to a man who was leading her down a road Omega knew well and had traveled down plenty of times. One that was naughty as sin.

"Now, can we get down to business and discuss the details of the party for next month, Riley?"

He shook his head. "No."

She lifted a brow. "No?"

He shook his head as he unbuttoned his coat to remove it and loosened his tie, tossing both on the chair across from his desk. "Not yet." Then, closing the distance between them, he pulled her into his arms.

She went to him willingly, opening her mouth the moment his lips touched hers. And when he slid his tongue inside, the memories of the last time they'd kissed magnified tenfold. She was convinced that no other man kissed the way he did. No other man could fill a woman with as much longing and desire as he could. Heat sizzled along her nerve endings, and her stomach tightened with each meticulous stroke of his tongue.

It was almost too late when she realized he had been walking her backward. Barely breaking the kiss, he eased her up by the hips to place her on top of his desk. He didn't let up, continuing to take her mouth with a hunger she felt in every part of her body. In response, she tightened her arms around his neck and moved in closer, needing the contact of his chest against hers, liking how her nipples were hardening in need.

"Mr. Westmoreland, I'm leaving for lunch now."

The sound of the receptionist's voice over the intercom seemed to boom across the room. Riley pulled his mouth away but kept it within inches of hers. "I hope you liked that," he whispered against her lips, tipping her chin up for better access.

A smile curved the corners of her mouth. "The kiss or the fact that your receptionist is taking lunch?"

He chuckled. "The kiss."

There was no reason to lie, so she said, "I did.""

He traced her lips with his tongue before saying, "Good. Just thought I'd get a little head start on all that pleasure I plan on giving you."

She thought he'd gotten more than a head start. "Do you mind getting me down off your desk now?"

"Not at all."

And just as easily as he'd placed her up there, he had her

back on her feet. They were standing close. She could feel the heat of him all over her. "I've got a suggestion, Alpha," he said in a deep, husky tone.

She lifted a brow. "What?"

"I suggest we move our meeting someplace else, and I know just the place. Go home and change into something comfortable—like jeans and boots—and I'll pick you up in an hour."

"And just where are we supposed to be going?"

"Riley's Station."

"Where?"

"Just do it, okay?"

"And this is a business meeting, right?"

A smile touched the corners of his mouth. "Both business and pleasure."

When she opened her mouth to remind him of her rules, he quickly spoke up and said, "I know, you want to take things slow and not be rushed. I got it."

She was glad he got it. Now if she could only get her traitorous body on the same page.

Six

Alpha tried keeping the butterflies from her stomach as she quickly dressed, knowing Riley would be there to pick her up in less than thirty minutes. "This is crazy," she muttered, pulling a burgundy V-neck sweater over her head. "All he had to say was 'let's go' and I'm going."

She stood sideways to look in the mirror at her perky breasts pressed against her sweater. It had been Omega's idea for her to wear a push-up bra with all her sweaters, and she would admit it made her girls look bigger than they really were.

She was about to put on lipstick when her cell phone rang. She grinned as she answered it. "Speak of the devil."

"Hey, and you were talking about me to who?" her sister said with laughter in her voice.

"No one, just thinking about what you told me, about ways a woman can make herself look sexy."

"Umm, you're trying to look sexy? Sounds like you've made some decisions about a few things."

Alpha leaned against the bathroom counter. When Omega had called last week she had spent over an hour on the phone telling her twin the latest about her meeting with Riley, how fine he was and his suggestion that they indulge in an affair. Of course Omega had been all for it, saying Alpha needed to rev up her love life. "Yes, I agreed to do it, and he's agreed not to rush me into anything."

"But no climax control, right?"

Alpha lifted a brow. "Climax control?"

"Yes, you plan to let the orgasms rip."

Alpha threw her hand to her mouth to keep from screaming with laughter. Her sister could be so outlandish at times. Um, in fact most of the time. "Behave, girl. And how is that book coming along?" Omega had decided to write a book about her experience as a porn star.

"Great. It's wonderful therapy for me."

Alpha didn't say anything for a minute and then asked, "Do you miss the business, Omega?" She'd always wondered but never asked. Nothing her parents said or did had made Omega give up her line of work until Omega had been ready to do so herself.

"I know it's hard for most people to understand, Al, but for me it was nothing more than a job—a job I needed while going through that rebellious period in my life. I don't want to think about where I'd be or what I'd still be doing if Marlon hadn't come along. He reminded me of who I was before I made those decisions, and he was willing to love me, no matter what."

Alpha loved her brother-in-law because she knew he loved Omega, no matter what her past had been. He didn't give a damn what others thought. He treated her sister like his queen.

Omega had been out of the business less than a year when she met Marlon. Alpha knew Omega was happy and could hear it in her voice every time they talked. The only dark cloud in her sister's life was their parents and their holier-than-thou attitude.

"The only thing I regret," Omega was saying softly, "is hurting you and the folks. Maybe one day they will forgive me. You never turned your back on me, even when the folks tried getting you to do so…and even when I cost you the man you loved because you wouldn't choose him over me."

Alpha nearly dropped the phone. "Who told you that? How did you know?" she asked, going back into the bedroom to sit on the edge of the bed. "I told you—"

"I know what you told me, and you lied. You and Eddie didn't just decide to call off the wedding because the two of you felt like you were drifting apart. I ran into Eleanor Sloan, in New York of all places, when Marlon took me there on a shopping spree. She approached me, thinking I was you, and you know Eleanor," Omega said of their high school friend. "She told me how sad she was for you now that Eddie had made you call off your wedding because of me."

Alpha tilted her head back and looked up at the ceiling. "When was this?"

"Last Christmas."

Alpha brought her head back down to gaze out the window and frowned. "And you've known all this time and never mentioned it," she accused. "Why *didn't* you mention it?"

Omega paused a minute before responding. "I couldn't say anything because I was feeling your pain. After the way I had lived those three years, here I was, about to marry the best man any woman could have, and there you were, you who'd always been the good girl and did everything the folks told you to do…even going to college for a career you didn't want to please them. I was the one who ended up with the fairy-tale marriage and getting a real prince and you ended up with a toad. It didn't seem fair. Life sucks."

A smile touched Alpha's lips. Life did suck at times, but a part of Alpha wouldn't change a thing. Because thanks to

Marlon, things were the way Alpha had always dreamed they could be for her twin.

Determined to get her sister back in a good mood, mainly because she didn't want Omega feeling sorry for her, Alpha said, "Yeah, must have been rough being a porn star."

"Oh, Alpha, you didn't have to go there."

She knew she'd succeeded in changing the mood when she heard the giggle in her twin's voice. Alpha laughed. "Yes, I did. Besides, had I been married to Eddie I wouldn't be having this fling and doing the no-climax-control thing."

Omega chuckled. "Okay, sis, you got me there. Is this Riley Westmoreland as hot as you make him out to be?"

Alpha remembered how he'd looked when she'd been to his office earlier that day. Yummy. "Trust me, he is. And I'll find out just how hot he is soon enough."

Omega went silent for a moment and then asked, "Will you tell him about me?"

She could hear the seriousness in her sister's tone. She had tried doing that with LeBron and Eddie and both men had ended up showing their true colors.

"Why would I tell him anything? It's not that kind of relationship. It's about sex and nothing more. Besides, at the point when we begin sleeping together, I doubt we'll have time for much pillow talk. Remember, no climax control. And I want to find out if multiple orgasms are real or something you porn stars just try to make look real."

Omega chuckled. "Oh, you're bad, and trust me, they are real...with the right man in control."

"We'll see. As far as being bad, I'm finally going to live a little, have some fun and enjoy myself. And I have a feeling Riley is just the person to make sure that I do so."

"Brrr. I can't believe the temperature has dropped five degrees already."

Riley smiled as he watched Alpha tighten her coat around

her when he escorted her to his truck and opened the door. "What are you complaining about, woman? It feels good out here."

She glared at him over her shoulder before easing into the truck's leather interior. "I can't help but wonder what kind of blood is running through your veins. Look at you."

He glanced down at himself. Okay, so he'd left his jacket in the truck. He looked fine. He felt fine. No sense reminding her he was hot-blooded. She would find the truth of that soon enough. He kept smiling as he closed the door and then rounded the front of the truck and opened the door to climb in on the driver's side. "I guess I've developed some sort of tolerance to Denver's cold weather."

After buckling up he smiled over at her and said, "My tolerance to Denver's cold weather drives everyone in my family crazy. They're convinced I'm going to die of pneumonia at an early age."

"I have to agree with them."

He tilted his head to look at her. "And you've been living in Denver for how long now?"

"It will be a year in April."

He grinned. "No wonder you're whining. You missed all the real good days."

"Lucky me. I'm not complaining," she said, chuckling. "If I had come any earlier I might have been tempted to head back south."

He glanced over at her. "You don't come across as a quitter, Alpha."

She chuckled. "I've thought of heading back south more than once, trust me."

As he was driving, he had to stop for a school bus. "I remember those days," he said thoughtfully.

"What days?" she asked.

He gestured with his head to somewhere outside the windshield. "When my brothers, cousin and I used to ride the bus to and from school. Either Aunt Susan or my mom would be there at the stop to get us. My parents had a van we all called Crazy Horse. It was blue and huge and could hold all of us."

"Sounds like a lot of good memories."

"They are."

"I admire you and your family, Riley," she said softly.

He looked over at Alpha. "Do you?"

"Yes. I heard about your parents and your uncle and aunt and how they died together in that plane crash. It must have been awful for all of you."

He stared straight ahead as his hand gripped the steering wheel and he watched the kids continue to unload from the bus. "It was, especially when there were so many of us still under sixteen. Seeing those kids reminds me of so many things. Kids think their parents are going to be around forever. I'll never forget the day I realized mine would not."

"How old were you?"

He glanced over at her. "Fifteen. Just a few months shy of my sixteenth birthday. Mom had promised me a party that year, and I was so looking forward to it. I had gotten my learner's permit, which meant I could start sharing Dillon's old truck with my brother, Jason. Life was good. Even Bane was good. He was my mom's baby. Spoiled rotten and a tattletale."

Riley was quiet for a second, remembering. "And then, suddenly all of it came to a crashing end, literally, when their plane went down. We lost them. Bane couldn't handle it and became a badass. He was hard for anyone to handle. Dillon was the oldest and then Ramsey. They had just finished college. Dillon was going pro in the NBA and Ramsey was on his way to Australia to learn about sheep ranching. They both gave up their dreams to keep our family together."

He felt her touch. Knew the moment she'd reached out and touched his arm. He needed the contact right then. Sad memories seldom came his way and when they did, they were too painful to dwell on. He'd been close to his mother, close to his father and aunt and uncle.

"Hey, you okay?"

He glanced over at Alpha. "Yes. Memories can be a bummer at times."

"Yes, I know."

He wondered if she was talking from experience. He had noted the indention on the third finger of her left hand where a ring used to be. Had she been married at one time? Deciding to change the subject, he said, "I thought about it and ran it over with the family. We're cool with the party being a black-tie affair. The reason I hesitated in making a decision was because I didn't want any of the employees to incur any unnecessary expenses if they didn't have to. But Dillon reminded me that this will be the company's fortieth holiday celebration so we need to be classy about it."

A huge smile touched her lips. "I was hoping that would be your decision. I like class and already have a lot of ideas on how to make the night special."

He nodded. "And they like the theme—One Winter's Night."

"That's great!"

When they came to a traffic light she opened her messenger bag to pull out several documents. "I have another presentation for you when we get to our destination. Now that you've decided on the attire, the menu can be planned accordingly. I'm working with Foods by Jerlon as the caterer."

"I've attended several parties he's catered, and everything he's prepared is delicious."

For the next half hour they covered more details about the party. It was only after discussing the budget that she lifted her gaze from her notes to look out the window. "We're a long way from town, aren't we?"

He glanced over at her. When had the sight of a woman with her hair in a ponytail ever turned him on? "Not too far."

He slowed the car to make a turn off the highway onto a two-lane road. A huge marker said Westmoreland Country.

She glanced over at him after reading the marker. "Westmoreland Country?"

He chuckled. "Yes. My great-great-grandfather settled here eighty-something years ago on over two thousand acres. Dillon, being the oldest, inherited the family home and the three-hundred acres it sat on. The rest of us got a hundred acres each once we turned twenty-five."

"So all of you stay around here, close together?"

"Close enough. Being on a hundred acres gives you privacy, at least most of the time, but there's still Bailey."

She raised a brow. "Bailey?"

"Bailey's my cousin and was the youngest Denver Westmoreland when my parents, uncle and aunt died. She likes to think she can boss all of us around. She hasn't reached twenty-five yet so she figures she can bum sleeping space wherever she wants. Usually she hangs out at Gemma's place since it's vacant now that Gemma is living in Australia."

"Is Gemma another cousin?"

"Yes." He decided it probably would be beneficial if he gave her a rundown of everyone. "On my parents' side there's Dillon. Then Micah, who works as a scientist for the federal government. He got married in June, and he and Kalina are expecting. Right now they're living in Alexandria, Virginia."

Riley slowed down when they reached another school zone. "Then there's Jason who's married to Bella." He chuckled. "She's from Savannah, and her first winter here was hard on her, too. Then there's me and my younger brothers, Canyon, Stern and Bane."

She lifted a brow. "No sisters?"

"Nope. I think my parents were hoping Bane was a girl, but it didn't turn out that way."

He then told her about his cousins, naming each one individually and the spouses of the married ones. Usually the last thing he talked about whenever he was on a date with a woman was his family. But he felt comfortable talking about them with Alpha.

He turned onto the road for his place and she glanced over at him and smiled. "Riley's Station?"

He chuckled. "Yes, Riley's Station."

Alpha was spellbound when they pulled into his yard. As far as the eye could see, she was surrounded by mountains and streams. Tucked away in the center of it all was a stately two-story house with a wraparound porch. Floor-to-ceiling windows covered the entire front of the house with a huge bay window facing the mountains on the side. A portion of the land close to the house had been cleared for a small waterfall and birdbath.

"All this is yours?" she asked, getting out of the car. He gripped her shoulders lightly when he placed his arms around her.

"Yes, one hundred acres. Isn't it beautiful?"

Beautiful? Words couldn't describe how soul-touchingly magnificent the view was. The one thing she had fallen in love with when she'd first visited Denver had been the mountains. Aside from the cold weather, Denver was a beautiful place.

"Now I understand about Riley's Station," she said, looking up at him.

"Do you?"

"Yes. On the way here I saw the markers—Ramsey's Web, Dillon's Den, Derringer's Dungeon, Zane's Hideout, Gemma's Gem…. Where on earth did those names come from?"

He threw his head back and laughed as he led her up the steps to the house. "Bailey. She figured all our places needed names and came up with them for us. She even designed the markers. At the time it was her pet project and we all gave in. We would have done anything to keep her out of trouble."

"I take it that she used to be a handful."

"If only you knew."

She stepped aside so he could open the door for her. "Welcome to my home, Alpha."

"Thanks," she said, passing him, stepping inside. For the second time that day her mouth almost dropped open. She moved from the foyer and glanced around at the open-concept room. His home was beautiful, the furnishings gorgeous and the decor breathtaking. The entire place was simply immaculate.

"Okay, although this is definitely a man's place, there's no way the decorating and coordinating of the furnishings was done by you. You hired an interior decorator, right?"

He moved away from the closed door. "Right. My cousin, Gemma. She owns an interior decorating company and insisted upon doing her thing in here."

Alpha continued to glance around. "Insisted."

"Yes, for the most part. I would have been satisfied just to have a kitchen table and a bed, but she'd made up her mind, after going into business for herself out of college, that her brothers and cousins would be her first clients. And none of us got discounts."

Alpha chuckled. "But I like that. Keeping it all in the family. Supporting one another."

"That's the Westmoreland Way." He moved across the room to open the blinds to a huge window that had a gorgeous, picturesque view of the mountains.

"And how do you keep it all clean and everything in place?" she asked, not seeing a speck of dirt or smidgen of dust anywhere.

His eyes glinted as if insulted. "Are you trying to insinuate I'm a slob?"

She waved off his pretended insult. "You're a man, Riley. Not too many tidy up after themselves. I'm impressed."

"Thank you, but I'll admit to having a weekly cleaning service. A woman drops by and takes care of the houses for all

the single Westmorelands. It's an annual birthday gift from
the ladies in the family for the single male Westmorelands."

He glanced at her messenger bag, which she was still carrying in her hand. "You can set up things in my office. I even
have a pull-down screen in there." He glanced at his watch.
"And while you're doing that, I'll start dinner."

She arched a brow. "You cook?"

He chuckled softly. "Yes, sweetheart, I learned how to fend
for myself when I discovered the women inviting me over to
their place to eat all had ulterior motives."

She tried ignoring the fluttering in the pit of her stomach
caused by his term of endearment as she eyed him up and
down. He had removed his jacket and tie and was standing in
the middle of his humongous living room, looking at home
and oh-so-sexy.

"Can you?"

"Can I what?"

"Cook," he said, opening blinds to another window.

"Yes."

"The kitchen is around that bend in the wall," he said.
"After getting things set up, you can join me and we'll see
how well you can cook."

When was the last time he'd whistled while cooking? Riley
wondered as he pulled all the spices he needed out of the cabinets. He glanced to where Alpha stood at the island making dessert—sugar cookies. She had come up with the idea
after discovering that he had all the ingredients she needed.

This wasn't the first time he'd ever invited a woman to his
house by any means, and this wasn't the first time one had
shared space in his kitchen. But he would admit, although
he didn't want to do so, that she was the first whose presence
felt totally right.

He pushed the thought to the back of his mind, not wanting to ponder why he felt that way. All he knew was that he

enjoyed glancing across the way and seeing her there. She was wearing a pullover sweater and a pair of skimmer jeans, and he liked the short leather boots on her feet. He thought the outfit was perfect for what he had in mind later. They were going horseback riding around his property after dinner.

A thought then entered his mind. "You do ride, right?"

She glanced over at him. "Ride what?"

"A horse."

She chuckled and the sound echoed around his kitchen. "Yes. I went to school to become a vet, remember. One year I spent the entire summer on a horse ranch in Ocala, Florida, working as a ranch hand. It was definitely a learning experience. I'm no jockey, but I can hold my own."

He stopped what he was doing and turned around. "Glad you think so because we're going riding later."

"We are?"

"Yes."

She shrugged. "Okay." She then returned to what she was doing.

"How are you coming along over there?" he asked, curious. She had been quiet, concentrating on the task until he'd interrupted her just now.

"Fine. You did preset the oven to 350 degrees, right?"

"Yes."

"Good. I haven't made sugar cookies in a long time. What are the odds that you would have everything I need?"

"Only because Bailey likes my kitchen and keeps it equipped."

She glanced up and around. "I can certainly see why she likes this one. It's a cook's dream. Beautiful oak cabinets, granite countertops, stainless steel appliances and—"

"Hey, you have all those things in your kitchen, except your cabinets are maple instead of oak."

"Yes, but I can place my small kitchen in here three or four times over. Most men would see this much square footage in a kitchen as wasted space."

"I'm not most men."

She glanced over at him and moved her gaze up and down. "Yes, I can see that."

He smiled and shook his head. "You know those kinds of looks can get you into trouble."

An innocent smile touched her lips. "I'm not doing anything."

Instead of disagreeing with her, he turned back around to the sink to start peeling the potatoes that he planned to stew on top of the stove with pork chops and his special gravy. The dish wasn't as good as McKay's, but he didn't think it was all bad.

Out of the corner of his eye he watched as Alpha opened his oven door to slide the tray of cookies inside. "These are slow-baking, so an hour should do it."

"I can't wait," he said, turning toward her. "Once I get this started it will be on simmer for a while."

"All right. Do you want me to cover the rest of the info for the party before or after dinner? The only thing left to cover is the budget."

He nodded. On the drive over she had covered a lot, being detailed and precise and, not surprisingly, he had liked all of her ideas. "Let's do it before dinner."

"Okay, I'll go get things set up in your office."

He watched her walk off with his pulse hammering and his erection throbbing. She looked good all over but had such a curvaceous backside that seeing her in jeans was a total turn-on for him.

Riley drew in a deep breath as the rush of blood seemed to hit him right in the groin. At some point they would share a bed, but he had promised not to rush her and he wouldn't, even if it killed him. Alpha was not a one-night stand, nor would she be a one-and-done. She would have her six weeks.

More importantly, he would have his six weeks. He doubted he would want less than that. And he'd taken the time earlier that day, while in his office, to figure out the exact ending date, and wouldn't you know it, it would be the night of the holiday party.

So it would be one winter's night in more ways than one.

Seven

"Well, what do you think about the pork chops?"

Alpha glanced across the table at Riley. It hadn't taken long to go over the budget and wrap up all the other minor details she needed to finalize in order to move ahead with her plans. All her people were ready and in place and now that he had approved her suggestions and the budget, it was full steam ahead. She'd be putting on a party that she knew would impress him and everyone attending.

She smiled ruefully. "I think if push comes to shove, you can quit your day job and become a chef. Everything tastes wonderful, Riley." And she meant it. The pork chops were so tender they all but melted in her mouth and the gravy and potatoes were better than any she'd ever eaten…even those at McKay's.

From his smile she knew her compliment pleased him. "Thanks. Wait until you taste my shrimp and lobster casserole. It's going to knock you off your feet."

Hmm, was that an invitation? Sounded like one to her. "I'll look forward to it."

"And I'm looking forward to eating your cookies. They smell good."

"Thanks."

She continued to eat and when she glanced up he was watching her with a strange look on his face. She tilted her head and arched a brow. "Something's wrong?"

"No," he said rather quickly and continued eating. Moments later, after taking a sip of his wine, he said, "I looked at a calendar earlier today and if we both agree to go the full six weeks for our affair, then it ends the night of the company party."

"Sounds good to me."

She saw something flash in his eyes. "So we understand each other?" he asked.

She smiled. "Perfectly." She then picked up her wineglass and took a sip, not sure why he was still sitting there staring at her. Had he expected her to request more time or something?

She glanced at her watch. It was getting late. She darted a look over at him. "Do you still want to go riding?"

"Yes.

"Then we need to get going if we want to take advantage of the daylight."

He stood. "I agree."

She stood, as well. "I'll help clear the table."

"You don't have to."

"I want to, and it's the least I can do for such a great meal. You outdid yourself."

He chuckled. "For you, any day."

She didn't say anything as she helped him clean off the table and load up the dishwasher. The heat was on, and it was getting to her already. And she had a feeling things would be getting hotter.

* * *

An hour later Riley stood at the window and looked out, waiting as Alpha used one of his guest bathrooms. He had enjoyed his time with her and now it was close to seven. It was hard to believe she had spent five hours with him today. And he had enjoyed every second of those hours. After dinner she had helped him clear the table and load the dishwasher. Then they had gone riding, and she'd pulled one over on him when she'd given the impression she wasn't good when it came to riding a horse. The woman was an excellent rider.

When they returned they had eaten the cookies she had baked and drunk cold glasses of milk. He shared more stories about his family and she had listened attentively, asking questions and laughing when he told her all about Bane's, Bailey's and the twins'—Aiden and Adrian's—escapades and how Family Services had threatened to separate the youngest Westmorelands from the family if their bad behaviors didn't improve.

But the one thing he noticed was that she hadn't talked a lot about herself or her family. He knew she was from Florida, that her parents owned a veterinary business and that she had a sister. But there was the issue of the missing ring on her finger. Had something other than a career move driven her to Denver?

"You even have a beautiful powder room, Riley. And it's so big. I probably could roll a bed in there and take a nap."

He turned around slowly. "Glad you—"

Whatever he was about to say died on his lips when their gazes connected. Suddenly, from across the room he held her in focus. His stomach tightened and his nerve endings sizzled. "Like it," he said, finishing his sentence.

She'd done something to her hair. It was no longer pulled back away from her face in a ponytail, but was now loose. A mass of brown curls were hanging around her shoulders. He'd seen her hair that way before, earlier today in his office.

But for some reason, at that moment, restyling her hair made her look incredibly beautiful.

His feet began moving toward her with a purpose ingrained in every part of his body. He met her gaze, held it, and when he came to a stop in front of her, he reached out and traced a finger across her chin. He then slowly moved his finger down the length of her neck before touching a lock of her hair. "You're wearing it differently," he said in a deep, husky voice, liking how the silky tresses felt flowing through his fingers.

She nodded slowly. "The clamp came loose while out riding and I thought I'd play it safe and take it off. The clamp was a gift from my sister and means a lot. I don't want to lose it."

"I like your hair this way. It's a stunning shade of brown. The color is perfect for your skin tone. It's beautiful. You're beautiful."

"Thank you."

He lifted her hands to his lips and kissed them while gazing up at her. "I promised not to rush you, but just so you know, I have no qualms about making love to you tonight. I'm tempted to do just that."

"Then I better move temptation out of your way by letting you take me home. Then you can concentrate on other things."

His lips curved in a smile. "Even if you weren't here, I would think about you, Alpha."

She chuckled softly. "I bet you say that to all the ladies."

Riley shook his head as he continued to kiss her hand. Now he was using the tip of his tongue to taste her skin. He liked hearing how her breathing sounded forced. "No, I don't say that to all the ladies."

And he meant that. He would admit to throwing out a convincing line or two when it served his purpose. That was to be expected when he was a man on the prowl. But that's not what he was doing here. With Alpha, he was being totally honest. He had thought about her over the past week more than he'd thought about any other woman. He had dreamed about her, waking up with a need and desire he'd never felt for any other woman.

Since he didn't know why his experience was so different with her, he intended to be cautious in whatever he did, whatever they shared. He had to be realistic enough to admit there had been something between him and Alpha from the first. She had been wearing gloves, yet when their hands touched he had felt the intense heat. He had felt the chemistry. An electrical charge had zinged through him. At first he'd thought it was a fluke, nothing more than an overreaction. But then, when he'd picked her up in his arms in McKay's parking lot to carry her into the restaurant, it was as if something had exploded between them, a connection he couldn't describe. And that was before he'd even seen what she was hiding under all those clothes.

He straightened and reached up to touch her chin again, coaxing her to meet his gaze. "Go out with me this weekend. We can do dinner and a movie or a play."

He studied the shape of her lips. Heat stirred his groin, making several ideas flow through his head and prompting him to add, "Or better yet, after dinner we can come here or go to your place and play a game."

Her brow arched. "What game?"

"The Pleasure Game. Have you ever played it before?"

He saw how her eyes darkened with desire when she shook her head. "Can't say that I have."

"Then let me assure you that you're going to enjoy it. It's easy to play, and there are not a whole lot of rules to follow. You can let me know that night if you want to play. How about if I pick you up for dinner around seven? There's this restaurant near the airport that I've heard nice things about, and I want to take you there."

"Okay," she said, smiling softly.

"And the Pleasure Game will require you staying overnight here or me staying overnight at your place. No pressure.

No rush. If you don't think you'll be ready to play Saturday night just let me know."

She nodded. "I will."

He leaned in close and slanted his mouth over hers, needing to taste her and leave her with something to think about. When she opened her mouth to return the kiss, he pulled her into his arms and deepened it, knowing he would be counting the days until he spent time with her again.

Eight

"Wow, the invitations will be simply beautiful," Lindsey Hopkins said. The twenty-something stay-at-home mom assisted Alpha on a part-time basis. As she looked at the computer screen over Alpha's shoulder, she had a huge grin on her face. "And you're the one designing them?"

Alpha smiled, too, pleased that Lindsey liked them. "Yes, after coming up with what I thought would work for our theme, One Winter's Night, I thought the idea of a country house in a light snowstorm would be perfect."

And she knew just the house she would use as a model. Riley's home. It would be picture-perfect. She had mentioned using a picture of his home on the invitation when he brought her home the other night. He said he had no problem with it and had given her the green light to do it.

"Do you know whose house you're going to use?" Lindsey asked her.

She turned her chair around and met Lindsey's inquiring

gaze. "Yes, it belongs to one of the Westmorelands. Riley Westmoreland."

Lindsey's face lit up. "He's one of Bane's older brothers. I met him once, and I bet the house is as gorgeous as he is."

Alpha threw her head back and laughed. "Well, yes, I guess you could say that."

"Trust me, I do. Every woman in town knows how good-looking those Westmoreland men are. Some of us are married, but we aren't blind. Any woman can appreciate a good-looking man."

Alpha grinned. "True." She turned back to the computer. "So you think Riley's house might work as a backdrop?"

"I've never seen it, but I don't see why not. I've been to Westmoreland Country once or twice, years ago with my father when he did the landscaping for the main house. He took me and my brothers along to help. You know, free labor," she said, laughing. "The main house was huge and majestic. I heard all the siblings have built their own homes now."

Alpha switched her computer to another screen, one that showed an example of some of the decorations she contemplated using. "Yes, that's what I heard." None of Riley's rules had governed publicizing their affair, but she didn't feel comfortable broadcasting it to anyone.

An hour or so later, Lindsey had left to pick up her baby from her mom and Alpha was on her way to the kitchen to fix a sandwich—her favorite, peanut butter and jelly—when the doorbell rang. Wondering who could be calling on her, she crossed the living room to the door. A quick glance out of the peephole indicated a florist deliveryman.

Pursing her lips thoughtfully, she opened the door. Who would send her flowers? Perhaps the man was at the wrong house. "May I help you?"

The older man smiled. "Alpha Blake?"

"Yes."

"These are for you," he said, handing her the huge, beautiful ceramic vase of pink roses. A dozen of them.

"Thanks," she said, accepting the flowers.

"And the tip has been taken care of."

"Oh, thanks," she said, stepping back and using her toe to close the door. The roses filled her house with a sweet-smelling scent. As soon as she set the vase down on the table, she pulled off the card, eager to see who'd sent them.

Two days left. Riley

She threw her head back and laughed. She had thought about everything he had suggested for Saturday night, especially the Pleasure Game, and felt she was ready. There was no need to put off the inevitable. Besides, she'd never played games with a man in the bedroom. Eddie hadn't had an imaginative bone in his body. LeBron had been full of ideas but only with the pretense that his bed partner was Omega. Alpha shook her head at how he actually hadn't seen anything wrong with wanting to make love to her while pretending she was her sister.

Moments later, Alpha was still standing in front of the table and gazing at the roses when her cell phone rang. She pulled it out of her pocket and saw it was her father. She and her parents talked at least once a week, but usually at night. She was surprised he was calling her in the middle of the day.

"Dad?"

"Yes, Al, how's my girl?"

She couldn't help but smile. "I'm fine. What about you?"

"Great. Look, I just had to call you and tell you I saw Eddie today when he brought Cleo into the office."

She frowned. "Is Cleo okay?" she asked, inquiring about the beautiful Labrador retriever that Eddie owned. She had fallen in love with the dog and had begun considering Cleo as hers, too.

"Yes, Cleo's fine. He brought her in for her annual visit."

"Oh. You didn't have to call to tell me that, Dad."

"I know, but I figured you'd want to know that he asked about you."

Like she cared. "Did he?"

"Yes. He even asked if you've mentioned anything about moving back home." There was a pause. Alpha knew she wouldn't like what was coming next but decided to let her father have his say since he would do so anyway.

"Look, baby, I know Eddie was the one to call off the wedding and all, but understand it from a man's point of view. He didn't want your reputation tarnished."

Alpha gritted her teeth. "He wanted me to disown Omega."

"But your sister chose the life she wanted. None of us were happy with it. Even your mom and I haven't been able to forgive her for embarrassing us that way."

And to this day Alpha felt her parents were wrong. She'd told them so more times than she could count. Regardless, Omega was their child and her sister, and nothing should have slid a wedge between those relationships. But her parents had succumbed to their friends' gossip and whispers. "I know, Dad, and you know how I felt about that. No matter what, she's still your daughter and my sister."

"Well, one day you're going to face up to what she did to us, what she did to you. You had men looking at you funny, thinking you were her."

"It was only one man, Dad." She had heard all this before and wasn't in the mood to rehash this with her father. "Besides, that was three years ago. Omega is now a happily married woman."

"With a past."

She rolled her eyes. "We all have one. Some a little naughtier than others."

"Naughtier? What your sister did was a disgrace."

"What Omega did has nothing to do with Eddie."

"Had you and Eddie married, the two of you would have been one, so it did have something to do with him. And as far as I'm concerned, he's a good man. All he wanted was to protect you."

"No. He was trying to control me."

There was a pause on the other end. "So you're saying the chances of the two of you getting back together are slim to none?"

"I'm leaning heavily on none."

There was another pause. "I hope you're not making a mistake. What about the next man you meet who might find out what your sister used to do for a living?"

"Any man I become seriously involved with, Dad, is going to have to accept me as I am. Omega has nothing to do with it."

"You're wrong, Al. She's a part of your past that you can't get rid of."

"No, Dad. She's a part of my present, and I can't imagine it being any other way."

When he heard the brisk knock on his office door, Riley knew who it was without looking up. "Come in, Canyon."

His brother entered, letting off steam. "Keisha Ashford is not the same woman I was involved with three years ago. Do you hear me, Ry? She is not the same woman."

Riley leaned back in his chair. "Yes, I hear you. In fact, I'm sure everyone on this floor heard you. I take it the meeting didn't go well?"

"Go well? That woman deliberately tried to make me look as if I didn't know what the hell I was doing."

A smile touched the corners of Riley's lips. He seldom saw his brother hot under the collar and just to know a woman was responsible was somewhat amusing. Especially since the Canyon he knew would never let a woman get under his skin. "And did you?" he asked, watching his brother angrily pace back and forth in front of his desk.

Canyon stopped and glared. "Did I what?"

"Know what the hell you were doing?"

At first Canyon appeared to have been taken aback by the question. But then he lifted his shoulders in a defensive stance. "Hell, yes, I knew what I was doing, but she deliberately tried to make me look bad."

Riley forced the smile off his face. "And why would she do something like that? Was it because she found out you were seeing another woman behind her back, when the two of you were supposed to be dating exclusively? Hmm?"

Canyon glared. "I was not seeing that other woman and you know it. Bonita Simpkins set me up, and Keisha fell for it."

Riley opened his mouth to say something but the receptionist's voice on the intercom stopped him. "Mr. Westmoreland, Ms. Alpha Blake is on line two for you."

"Thanks." He then glanced over at his brother. "I need to take this call."

His brother shrugged. "Go ahead."

When Canyon just stood there, apparently still fuming over his encounter with Keisha, Riley cleared his throat and said, "It's a private call."

Canyon lifted a brow. "With the company's event planner? What could be so private about that?"

When Riley didn't respond but continued to sit and stare at his brother, waiting for him to leave, something flickered in the dark depths of Canyon's eyes. "Please don't tell me you've got the hots for the event planner."

"Okay, I won't tell you. Close the door behind you on the way out."

Canyon stood there and gaped at him. "I don't believe it."

Riley rolled his eyes. "What don't you believe?"

"What happened to your policy about never mixing business with pleasure?"

"It's still in place. I'm not mixing them. When we conduct business, we conduct business. And when we want pleasure, we'll have pleasure. Solely separate entities that aren't being mixed."

Canyon threw his head back and laughed. "You sound like a damn politician who's breaking the rule and then trying to find a way to make the situation work for you."

"Goodbye, Canyon. If I were you, I would focus on a way to make peace with Keisha Ashford."

The amusement on Canyon's face immediately vanished to be replaced with a glare. "You take care of your business, and I'll take care of mine."

It was on the tip of Riley's tongue to tell his brother that he was the one who sought him out and not the other way around. "Whatever."

It was only after Canyon had left and closed the door behind him that Riley clicked on the second line. "Alpha? Sorry for the wait."

"No problem. I'm just calling to thank you for the flowers. They are beautiful."

So are you. "I'm glad you like them."

"I do. I truly do."

He leaned back in his chair and did something he hadn't done in a long time—propped his feet up on his desk. "So, what have you been doing with yourself since I last saw you?" *Which was only two days ago.*

"Designing the invitations, picking up items for decorating and finalizing the menu with the chef. However, I did take time out for my dance classes."

He lifted a brow. "You're taking dance classes?"

She chuckled. "Yes, twice a week at the high school at night."

Why didn't he know that? And just as quickly as he thought it, he was reminded that their connection was about sex without commitment. There was no need for him to know what she did every hour of the day. "Sounds like fun."

"It is. Well, I don't want to hold you up. I just wanted to call and thank you for the flowers and to let you know how beautiful they are."

"You're welcome and have a good night." He paused a moment and then said in a low tone, "Think about me tonight."

"I will. We have two more days."

He drew in a long and deep breath, already feeling frustration settle within his bones. Two days was too long in his book. "Yes, we have two days."

It was hard not to suggest they shorten that time. He could drop by later. But he would hold fast and not give in to temptation. He had offered this time before their date on Saturday because he wanted it to be special for her. However, he decided to say, "I can't wait to see you again. I've thought of you often."

"And I've thought of you often, as well."

That was good to hear, but he doubted she had thought of him as much as he'd thought of her. It had been hard to concentrate on all the reports that had come across his desk and not on the memories of her and that night they'd dined together at his place. Whether it was the dinner they'd shared, the conversation between them or the horseback ride they'd taken, he had enjoyed his time with her, and there hadn't been anything sexual about it. Just sitting across from her, admiring the soft and smooth skin of her face, the stunning bone structure that made her such a gorgeous woman, the pair of lips he could get addicted to if not careful…

"Goodbye, Riley."

"Goodbye."

He eased his legs off his desk to stand and walk over to the window. He and Canyon had tossed for this office, mainly because of the view. There was snow on the top of the mountains and already he felt the urge to go skiing. He had a trip planned to Aspen in January and wondered if Alpha could ski.

He shook his head, chuckling at the foolish thought. She couldn't stand cold weather so chances were she would never venture anyplace where snow was waist-deep and you could feel the cold all the way to the bones.

But the most important thing he had to remember was that his affair with Alpha would be over by then.

For some reason that thought bothered him.

Nine

Saturday night hadn't come quickly enough, Alpha thought, standing in front of the full-length mirror to give herself a final once-over. She had appreciated the good weather yesterday since it had given her the chance to go shopping. This was her first official date with Riley and she wanted to wear everything new—from the inside out.

This is when she missed Omega the most. As teens, and even while in college, they would go places and do things together, especially shopping. They'd shared some of the same taste in clothing and shoes, but when it came to undergarments, Omega was always more daring.

Alpha looked down at her legs. It would get colder later so she'd decided to wear a pair of boots, a new black suede pair she had bought yesterday. She liked the way they fit her legs, but more importantly, she liked how they looked with the outfit she was wearing—a printed kimono top with an elastic belt that emphasized her small waistline and a black sateen pencil skirt that highlighted her boots.

Her hair was styled slightly differently after her visit to a salon yesterday morning. She knew Riley liked seeing her hair around her shoulders, since he'd said as much that night at his place. So she had enhanced the look by making her hair appear fuller. She'd gotten it layered around her shoulders. A number of people had complimented the new style and said it was perfect for her face.

Riley had suggested that they either spend the night at his place or here, and either one was fine with her. She was so looking forward to tonight and a part of her felt giddy. Omega had called earlier that day and suggested she have an overnight bag packed just in case.

And because there was a chance this is where they would end the evening, her bedroom was ready. She had even bought silk sheets for her bed and scented candles had been placed all around. She liked the way her bedroom looked and although it wasn't nearly as large as Riley's, it would serve their purpose.

As she moved away from the mirror, she recalled the tour Riley had given her of his home. Why one person would need that much space she didn't know. But she had to admit there was something about every room that suited him.

Even his entertainment room suited him. Or should she say *rooms,* since there were two. There was a state-of-the-art theater with power-operated reclining seats. His music room held a white oak entertainment system with a sophisticated stereo, and a beautiful white Steinway baby grand piano sat in the middle of the floor. According to Riley, his mother, who had been a music major in college, had taught each of her seven sons how to play the piano. After she'd died, Dillon had made sure the lessons continued by hiring a private music instructor.

Alpha's heart kicked up a notch when she heard the ringing of the doorbell. A quick glance at her watch indicated Riley was fifteen minutes early.

She glanced around her bedroom one last time, liking what

she saw. Her queen-size bed was covered in a beautiful blue comforter and she'd added additional shams and decorative pillows. She'd changed the wattage of the lightbulbs in the lamps on both sides of her bed to soften the lighting in the room. Her bedroom had been transformed into a romantic haven.

She liked it. She liked it a lot. And she hoped that if Riley got the chance to see it, he would like it, as well.

"I hope I'm not too early, but I wasn't sure how traffic would be coming this way," Riley said, once he'd been able to regain control of his senses. He had almost lost them when Alpha opened the door. She looked absolutely stunning, from the new hairstyle she was sporting to the outfit she was wearing. Sexy enough to devour. She hadn't called to say she wasn't ready for the Pleasure Game later so he could only assume that she was.

Raw need, mingled with potent lust, consumed him. His body hadn't wasted time getting aroused. This was one time he was grateful for the long leather coat he was wearing. But his full concentration was on what *she* was wearing. Her outfit was designed to articulate every curve on her body and was doing a great job.

"No, you're not too early at all. It will only take a second to grab my coat," she said, stepping aside so he could enter her home.

"Take your time, Alpha."

"Thanks."

And then, with deep male appreciation, he watched her walk off, getting even more aroused by the sway of her hips with every step she took in that pencil skirt with the slit in the back. When she was no longer in sight, he drew in a deep breath, knowing it would be one of those kinds of nights. The only good thing about knowing it was being fully aware of how it would end.

He would let her decide whose bed they would sleep in tonight. It didn't matter to him since he didn't intend for them to get much sleep. That was why he intended to feed her well because she would definitely need all her energy for later.

"I'm ready, Riley."

That made two of them. He was ready, as well.

"I guess now is the time to ask whether I'll be coming back here tonight," she said. He saw the flash of color that appeared in her cheeks and knew the topic of what they intended to do later made her blush. He smiled thinking that she would be doing a whole hell of a lot of blushing later, if she had any shy bones in her body.

He shoved his hands into his coat pockets. "It's your decision. It doesn't matter to me where we make love."

His bluntness caused the color in her cheeks to deepen, but that did nothing for the heated look she gave him from beneath her silky long lashes. He knew it was unintentional, but nobody informed his erection, which was beginning to throb like hell. When she nervously licked her lips, he knew that if he didn't get her out of there now he would be initiating a roll on the floor in the next few minutes.

"I'd like to come back here," she said softly, holding his gaze.

"Then we shall. Ready?"

She nodded and led him to the door for them to leave. As far as he was concerned, it wasn't a moment too soon.

"Welcome tonight, Mr. Westmoreland. Your table is ready."

"Thanks, Pierre," Riley said, handing his coat to the manager of the restaurant.

While Riley assisted Alpha in removing her coat, she thanked the older man, who had a deep French accent, a Maurice Chevalier reincarnated. He gave her a brilliant smile, leaned in and lifted her hand to kiss the back of it. "Welcome to *Les' Amores, mademoiselle.* You are most beautiful."

She smiled at the compliment. "Thank you."

He straightened and then grabbed a couple of menus from a nearby rack. "Please follow me."

Alpha glanced at her surroundings as they followed their host. She had been quite taken with the French restaurant the moment Riley had turned into the courtyard of fine shops and boutiques. Since moving to Denver she had heard about *Les' Amores* but had never had the opportunity to dine at the plush brasserie.

As Pierre led them through the main dining area, she took note of the adobe brick walls lined with ornamental racks filled with fine wine and crystal glasses. The tables were adorned with red silk tablecloths and candle lanterns. Authentic French artwork hung on the walls and a large fireplace with a roaring blaze was in the middle of the room.

Instead of seating them at one of the vacant tables they passed, Pierre escorted them to a room in the back that had a table set for two. The room was quaint with wooden beam ceilings and a huge brick fireplace. Cozy and private.

Riley moved to pull out her chair before Pierre had a chance to do so and leaned close to her ear to whisper, "I love your outfit, but I can't wait to take it off you." She couldn't help the blush that crept into her features. She knew he was telling her that the seduction of Alpha Blake had begun.

He took his chair and Pierre handed them menus and proceeded to offer his recommendations for that night. That done, he asked about wine and Riley named a brand she'd never heard of. When she looked at him, he turned sensual dark eyes on her and said, "It's a magnificent blend. You'll like it."

She nodded, swallowing deeply and wondering if she would need something stronger to get her through the evening. "I'm sure I will."

Pierre left them and within minutes was back to pour their

wine. "I'll give you time to look at the menu," he said, easing from the room and leaving them alone.

Alpha glanced down at the menu. "Everything looks good, Riley. What do you recommend?"

"About you or what's on the menu?" he asked with a flirty wink at her.

She gave him an admonishing smile, wondering if this was how it would be for the rest of the night. "The menu, Riley."

He smiled. "In that case I would recommend the…"

She listened while he rattled off a number of dishes, pronouncing each in a deep French accent that stirred her nerve endings. She gazed deep into the eyes staring back at her. In the depths of his dark gaze was a promise of what would come later. A hot, lusty night filled with pleasure. And heaven help her, she was looking forward to it.

"So what do you think, Alpha?"

She knew he was asking about the menu and the dishes he'd just told her about, but though she had heard, she hadn't listened. "I'll let you decide."

He nodded and gave her a smile, one that told her he knew why she was taking the easy way out. Pierre returned with the wine and poured some into their glasses and then took their orders. When he left, Alpha glanced around.

The room was small and intimate. They had been given a table with a view of Pikes Peak, and it was breathtaking. Music was flowing into the room through hidden speakers, and the tunes were romantic. She hadn't realized how secluded the room was until she recalled walking through the restaurant to get to it. Not only did the fire blazing in the fireplace provide warmth, but it also set an intimate tone. On the drive over, she'd tried bringing him up to date on the party plans, but Riley had reached out, touched her hand and said tonight was not about the party but about them.

"This is a nice room," she said.

"I'm glad you like it. So tell me, Alpha. Do you ski?"

* * *

Why was he asking her that? Riley immediately wondered. It had to be for the purpose of conversation, nothing more. The inquiry certainly couldn't have anything to do with his ski trip to Aspen in January since their affair would have ended by then.

"No, I don't ski."

He wasn't surprised. "Would you like to learn how?"

She shook her head. "That would mean being out in not just cold weather but super cold weather, so I'll pass."

He should let it go, but couldn't. "What if I promised to keep you warm?"

She chuckled. "I don't think you can keep me *that* warm, Riley."

"But if I could?" he inquired further, taking a sip of his wine.

"You can't."

He didn't say anything but, deep down, he saw it as a challenge. He held her gaze. "We'll see."

She tilted her head and looked at him. "Tell me. What do you get out of skiing? I heard it's not really a form of exercise."

He watched her take a sip of her wine. The way she closed her lips around the mouth of the glass sent flutters off in his stomach. "Not true. Any time you use muscles you don't normally use, you're exercising."

He took a sip of his wine as he told her about the first time he'd put on a pair of skis. "I was all but seven and my father and uncle took their sons on a ski trip for the sole purpose of providing us with professional ski lessons."

He chuckled. "I guess they knew their sons and figured if they didn't make sure we were taught by a professional then we would learn the wrong way and risk our lives. Being on the slopes with my family was special to me and I consider those memories some of the best ones of my childhood. Maybe that's why I enjoy skiing so much."

He saw the wistful look that shone in her eyes, so he added, "I'm sure you and your sister did things with your family that you hold as special memories, too."

She shifted her gaze from his to pick up her glass of wine. "Yes, of course."

Not for the first time, he thought she was deliberately not sharing information about her family. It shouldn't bother him, but it did, mainly because he didn't have any problem telling her about his family. The only thing he knew about her parents was that they had wanted her to go into veterinary medicine but had accepted her decision to change careers. She seldom mentioned anything about her sister, and he could only assume the two were not close. And he was still curious about the ring that used to be on her finger. He was about to question her on the topic when Pierre returned with their appetizers.

Pierre, efficient as ever, was in and out in no time, leaving them alone once again with a basket of hot buttered rolls, a platter of imported French escargots sautéed in a creamy, garlic butter sauce and steamed artichoke. He'd even taken the time to refill their wineglasses before breezing out.

Riley glanced over at Alpha. He should have used the time during Pierre's interruption to rethink pursuing his interest in the man who'd put a ring on her finger, as well as the reason she didn't talk much about her family, but he didn't. For some reason, he felt the need to address it. "Can I ask you something?"

She was reaching for an escargot and glanced over at him with a smile. "Just as long as what you want to ask has nothing to do with these. They look delicious."

He chuckled. "Not at all, please help yourself," he said, glad she was enjoying his choice in foods.

"Okay, then, ask away."

"I have two questions, really. I noticed you used to wear a ring. Were you married before?"

Her hands stilled. "Does it matter?"

He held her gaze and shook his head. "No. I'm just curious."

"No, I've never been married, but up until a year ago I was engaged."

"What happened?" he asked, as if he had every right to know.

She didn't say anything for a minute and then, "It was decided that marriage wasn't the right move for us after all."

She was being somewhat evasive so he couldn't help wondering who had made that decision. The guy? Her? Had it been mutual? Why did he care? It didn't matter, and he only cared if she'd gotten hurt by the decision. But, in a way, he was glad the marriage didn't take place because if it had she wouldn't be here with him tonight.

"And your second question?" she asked, returning to eating.

He smiled. She was letting him know there wouldn't be any further discussion on the first question. "Why don't you like talking about your family?" Her hands stilled again, and he could tell she was about to freeze up on him, but he refused to let her do that.

"I told you about my family, Riley."

"Not enough."

"I told you my parents were veterinarians in Daytona and that I have a sister."

"Is she still alive?"

She lifted a brow. "Who?"

"Your sister."

"Yes. Why do you ask?"

He shrugged. "Because you never talk about her. Where does she live? Is she married? Does she have any kids?"

Something, he wasn't sure what, flashed in her eyes before

she lowered her head to slowly bite into an escargot. "Omega lives in Paris. She's married to a wonderful man and they are trying real hard to start a family."

"Are the two of you close?"

"Yes, very close. As close as any two sisters can be."

His curiosity had been appeased. He decided that, in the future, the subjects of her ex-fiancé and her family were closed unless she brought them up. "You like that?" he asked, motioning to the escargot she had gone back to eating. He was getting turned on as he watched her chew a few times and then lick her lips.

"Yes, it's delicious."

A trickle of butter was running down her chin. "Come here and lean close," he told her, picking up his napkin to wipe away the butter. But when she leaned in toward him, he changed his mind and swiped the butter from her chin with the tip of his tongue.

"There," he said huskily. As he drew back, he met the surprised look in her eyes and smiled. "It's all gone now."

"Thanks," she murmured softly, drawing back in her chair.

"Anytime. I like the way you taste," he responded huskily.

She took a sip of her wine. "It was the butter."

A doubtful smile curved his lips. "Umm, the butter tasted good but you tasted better. Makes me anxious to taste you all over later."

Riley watched as a blush touched her cheeks and she took another sip of her wine. "Don't drink too much of that, baby. I want your mind completely functional for later."

"Will that be all, Mr. Westmoreland?" Pierre asked after he and another waiter finished clearing the table. He had already asked if either Riley or Alpha wanted dessert and they had both declined.

"No, Pierre, that will be all. Just make sure we aren't disturbed for the remainder of the evening."

"Yes, sir." The older man quickly left with the other waiter trailing behind him.

No sooner had the door closed than Alpha swore she heard the distinct sound of a lock clicking in place, and Riley turned his full attention to her. His dark, piercing eyes held her within their scope and she all but squirmed in her seat, feeling sexual currents flow from him. Suddenly, an electrical charge seemed to vibrate through the air causing blood to rush through her veins.

Blood was rushing through another area of her body, as well, the one located at the juncture of her thighs, which made her cross her legs. She drew in a slow breath when he stood and rounded the table. Holding out his hand, he said, in what sounded like a deep, husky growl, "Dance with me."

Alpha felt her stomach quiver with each word he said. Earlier, she had heard music flowing into the room but the sound had been rather faint. At that moment, as if on cue, the volume increased. She slipped her hand into his, feeling his heat immediately. Uncrossing her legs, she eased from her chair and he gently pulled her into his arms, right smack against his hard, masculine body.

The song being played was perfect, just the right tempo for the way their bodies melded together as they swayed to the lyrics and melody. With her hand on his shoulder and her head lying on his chest, she could feel the rapid beat of his heart, which was somehow keeping time with hers. Being this close to him, bodies locked as tightly as they could be, stirred something elemental in her blood and reminded her of just how potent the chemistry was between them.

Pressed against him, she felt every inch of his lean strength. And when his hips moved, so did hers, slowly, methodically, magnetically. Heat sizzled through all parts of her when she felt his hard erection against her middle. The pressure triggered her nipples to harden. An ache began in her loins and branched upward, filling her with an indescribable hunger, a sexual need she didn't know she was capable of feeling.

"You okay?"

The sound of his voice ignited rampant sensations within her. She raised her eyes to his and inwardly moaned when she connected to the dark depths. "Yes, I'm okay." *But barely,* she held off saying. Never before had dancing with a man caused this much havoc on her emotions. Never had it driven her to want things she'd never wanted before.

They continued to gaze into each other's eyes as they swayed to the music. When one song moved to another, they stood in the same spot, feet firmly planted, bodies barely moving while his hand spanned her backside, making a slow ache throb there. She reveled in the feel of him holding her in his arms.

When she couldn't take looking into his eyes any longer, she placed her head on his chest again. The heat from his gaze was unnerving her, making it hard for her to breathe. What was there about him that made her not want to fight the heat but to wallow in it? She wanted tonight. She needed tonight—and all the nights he wanted to give her…for six weeks. And when it was over, it would be over. Final, with no regrets, no worrying about a lost love that should last forever or a love that never was. She was going into this affair with her eyes wide open. She was not the naive woman who'd thought she was the luckiest female on earth when Edward Swisher, of the prestigious Daytona Swishers, had asked her out. She had learned her lesson. She should have learned it with LeBron. But it had taken Eddie to make her vow never to give her heart to another man.

The song melded into another and they continued dancing. He tightened his arms around her and held her closer. Her breath caught each and every time he would deliberately slide his leg between hers, letting her feel the length of him through his pants. She could feel her panties getting wet with each moment of contact.

Almost overwhelmed in desire, she tilted her head back, met the dark, penetrating gaze staring down at her and asked, "What are you doing to me?"

He didn't even pretend not to know what she was asking. "Prepping you for later."

Who needed to be prepped? She opened her mouth to ask him that very thing when he lowered his mouth to hers, slid his tongue inside and proceeded to kiss her in a way that sent powerful surges through her. He began toying with her tongue, feasting on it like a hungry man getting his last meal.

She was just as greedy when she tightened her arms around him while they devoured each other's mouths. Nothing else mattered at that moment. It meant nothing to her that they were in a public place and there were people on the other side of that door having dinner. Nor did it matter that Pierre and that other waiter probably had a good idea what she and Riley were doing in here. All that mattered at the moment was the way he was kissing her, stirring a need within her that was nearly making her lose it.

Riley pulled his mouth back, and she was able to draw in a much-needed breath. He was able to do the same and rested his forehead against hers.

"Baby, I should be the one asking what *you* are doing to me," he whispered softly against her lips that were still moist from their kiss. "All I want to do at this moment is put you on that table and spread you wide and take you like I've been dreaming of doing for the past couple of weeks."

Her heartbeat kicked up a notch, knowing he wanted her as much as she wanted him. She refused to play games about this. She wanted to experience it all, and she wanted to experience it with him. She wanted several nights of hot, mind-blowing sex with no strings attached and no guilty conscience to deal with afterward.

She would go into the affair as the consenting and mature adult she was. She was the one paying the bills on Noble Lane, and what she did there was nobody's business, certainly not her parents', who lived thousands of miles away. They would frown upon an affair between her and anyone. Her father was hoping that she and Eddie would get back together even if it meant she would have to cut ties with her twin sister to do so.

"Are you ready for me to take you home?"

His question gave her pause. Now would be the perfect time, if she wanted to change her mind about anything they planned to do later. But her mind was made up, and she wasn't changing it. "Yes, I'm ready."

He pulled back slightly and looked at her, those dark eyes locked with hers, refusing to look away, as if her very soul was laid out for him to read like a book. "Are you sure you're ready, Alpha? I intend for it to be one hell of a night."

And she was counting on just that. She nodded, deciding right then and there to shed her inhibitions once and for all. She countered his question with one of her own. "Maybe I should be asking you the same thing, Riley. Are you sure you're ready?"

He reached down, took her hand and led it to the crotch of his pants. "What does that tell you?"

Oh, he was ready all right. What he'd done by letting her touch him was a bold move, one Eddie would never have taken. Eddie would never have encouraged her to cop a feel. And since Riley put her hand there, she saw no reason to move it…at least not yet. She was simply amazed how large he felt behind his zipper. She moved her hand around to take in the length, shape and feel of him.

"If you keep it up, Alpha, I just might be tempted to take you here and now."

Something, she wasn't sure what, drove her to utter her next words. "Do it."

"What did you say?" he asked, his voice deep and throaty, his eyes steady, mesmerizing and hungry.

She could play it off and pretend she hadn't said anything. But she didn't want to do that. What would be the point? She wanted Riley, and she wanted him now.

Alpha leaned in close to him and whispered, "I said, do it. Do it now."

She could tell from the way his breathing changed that he got the message. "Then take it out," he whispered against her lips. "You want it, then go in and get it, baby."

Her heartbeat kicked up another notch. His gaze held hers as she slowly eased down his zipper and then reached inside the opening. She tried releasing him but found his briefs to be in the way.

After a few failed efforts, he asked, "Need help?"

She didn't see amusement in his gaze, just gut-wrenching need. "Yes. Please."

He took one step back, and she watched as he pulled himself out of his pants. She sucked in a deep breath when she saw him and her mouth nearly dropped open. He was huge and had a condom in hand.

"Don't tempt me with an open mouth, baby," he said, easing on protection.

She closed it, and before she could think about anything, he moved back toward her. "Now lift up your skirt for me, Alpha."

She slowly inched up her skirt, giving him a view of her silk thigh-high stockings and lacy black panties. She wasn't sure what he'd planned to do next, but she hadn't expected him to reach out and tug her panties past her knees and down her legs.

"That's what I want to see," he said, staring at the throbbing flesh her panties had been hiding. "It's just like I thought it would be. You look beautiful there, and your color is natural."

Alpha swallowed hard. "Yes, of course. I've never dyed my hair."

As if seeing that part of her bared wasn't enough, he reached out and touched her, trailed fingers through the curls and all around her feminine folds, slipping one finger inside as if to test her wetness. Her legs automatically parted to give him better access. And he took it, penetrating his finger farther inside of her.

She heard him draw in a deep breath before he said, "Your scent is killing me." And when he removed his finger from inside of her and inserted it between his lips to suck on it, she got weak in the knees.

"And you taste good, too. I'm having you for breakfast in the morning."

Before she could figure out if he was serious or teasing, his hands went to her waist and he lifted her off her feet. "Wrap your legs around me," he instructed huskily.

She did so and the moment he lifted her body, she felt the head of his erection touch her. Easing her legs apart a little more, she sucked in hard when he thrust inside of her, clutching tight to her hips until he was fully embedded within her. She wasn't aware a man could go that deep.

"Now we dance this way," he said against her moist lips.

And they did. While the music played, he held her in his arms with her legs wrapped around him, supporting her weight while he was fully planted inside of her. She tightened her arms around his neck, swiveling her hips against him in tiny circles, keeping a sensuous beat with the music. Never had she danced with a man like this before. Rocking his body hard against hers and reminding her of just how buried he was inside of her. The intense penetration combined with the moves of their bodies to stimulate her with searing intensity. She closed her eyes as her nerve endings became more and more charged. Electrified. Intensified.

And then there was the scent of him, clean and masculine.

Whatever cologne he was wearing was a fragrance meant to drive a woman over the edge, and it was definitely doing a number on her. His hold on her thighs tightened even more, and the next thing she knew there was a hard wall against her back. She hadn't been aware they had moved away from that spot in the center of the room.

"I can't take you slow anymore," he growled seconds before he began thrusting in and out of her hard and fast, working his hips back and forth and side to side. She tightened her legs around him, convinced he was trying to drive her insane.

When she felt her body about to explode, she moaned his name and was just about to scream when his mouth lowered and planted firmly on hers.

But that didn't stop her body from splintering into a thousand pieces. And she knew the moment his detonated, as well. He thrust deeper, harder and she felt him, all the way to her womb. Her muscles squeezed him, were driven to hold him hostage inside of her.

This was incredible. He was incredible.

She reveled in the feel of his body in hers, the hardness of his chest against hers and how his firm, muscled thighs felt while keeping her propped up against the wall. She fought not to scream again but couldn't retain it, and once again his mouth was there to silence her.

Moments later, when he pulled his mouth away, dark eyes stared into hers and she read what his eyes were saying. *I want more.*

She mouthed her response. *Get all you want.*

He remained inside of her, staring down at her, until they were both able to breathe normally again. It was only then that he lowered her feet to the floor and leaned down to pull up her panties before rearranging her skirt, smoothing it over her hips and thighs. She then watched as he proceeded to tuck himself back inside his pants.

After rezipping, he glanced over at her. "Ready to go play Pleasure Games?"

"I'm more than ready," she said, as a satisfied smile touched her lips, although she wasn't sure just where she would find the energy to do such a thing.

He returned her smile. "I'll instruct Pierre to bring our coats. The sooner I get you to your house, the better."

Funny, she'd been thinking the same thing.

Ten

Riley had a tough time maintaining his self-control on the drive to Alpha's home mainly because she was deliberately making it hard for him. Instead of using his truck, he was driving his Lexus sports car. It was sleek and smooth and perfect for the classy woman sitting beside him. However, the car's intimacy was almost more than he could handle, especially since her scent was all over the place.

He glanced over at Alpha, knowing he should be keeping his eyes on the road. But he was finding it hard to do so when she was deliberately inching up her skirt to show a pair of luscious brown thighs. It didn't take much to remember how it felt being between those thighs, which made his erection hard with the anticipation of getting between them again.

He had enjoyed sharing dinner with her, had loved sitting across from her and watching her mouth move as she ate. Not for the first time, his head had been filled with thoughts of all the things he would love to see that mouth do to him.

But he would also admit he had enjoyed their conversation. Although he had pretty much gotten the hint that her past was not open for discussion, and he had told her early on that he didn't want them to discuss anything about the party, they had managed to find other things to talk about. Mainly movies they had seen, their thoughts about the ongoing war, the recent election and Hollywood scandals. He had been surprised to discover they had the same tastes and opinions about a number of things.

He'd also told her about his cousins in Atlanta, Texas and Montana, and how excited the family was about his cousin Megan's upcoming wedding in June, which meant the family would all be getting together again. And he shouldn't have been surprised when Alpha told him that Megan was considering her as a wedding planner and had interviewed her last week. Megan would be making her decision in a couple of weeks.

He told her about his great-grandfather, Raphel, and how Megan had hired a private investigator to find information about him, and how the two traveled to Texas to discover Raphel had a child before marrying Riley's great-grandmother, which meant the possibility of more Westmorelands somewhere.

He glanced around when traffic slowed down. He had decided to drive through town to hit the interstate, figuring there wouldn't be much traffic tonight. But that assumption had turned out to be wrong when he got caught up with people leaving a concert.

To get out of the mad rush he had taken another shortcut that carried him through another part of town known for its boutiques. Thanksgiving was just a few weeks away and already storefronts were all decked out for Christmas.

Riley glanced over at Alpha's thighs again. She had hiked up the hem of her skirt another inch or two. He loosened his tie when he brought the car to a traffic light and frowned over at her. "Be forewarned, Alpha. If tempted badly enough

I wouldn't hesitate to pull this car to the side of the road and take you again, here and now."

She threw her head back and laughed as if she couldn't imagine such a thing. The sound flowing from her throat stirred his blood and sent it straight to his groin.

"That should make interesting reading in the newspapers tomorrow morning if the sheriff or one of his deputies stumbles upon us," she replied smartly.

He held her gaze intensely. "Trust me, it won't make the papers. Dillon is best friends with Sheriff Harper and it wouldn't be the first Westmoreland he's come across on the side of the road."

She tilted her head. "Do tell. Is it something that runs in the family?"

He chuckled. "Only with Bane. I can't tell you the number of times Sheriff Harper brought Bane home after coming across him and Crystal parked somewhere."

"Crystal?"

Riley frowned. "Yes, Crystal Newsome, Bane's obsession. Maybe I should say they were equally obsessed with each other."

He decided to keep talking, figuring it would take his mind off getting under her skirt. "Crystal and Bane have been under each other's skin since they were kids. It would drive Mr. Newsome bonkers, not just because Bane was four years older than Crystal but because Crystal told anyone who wanted to listen—and even those who didn't—that she wanted Bane and vice versa, even when they were too young to think about wanting anyone. Mr. Newsome was totally against a union between his daughter and a Westmoreland."

"Why?"

He shrugged. "Something that happened years ago with our grandfathers, resulting in a grudge that ran deep. It was unfortunate for Crystal and Bane."

"What happened?" Alpha asked curiously.

"Carl Newsome got tired of Crystal climbing out of her bedroom window in the dead of night or cutting school just to be with Bane. Since Crystal was a minor, at fifteen, and Bane was nineteen, old man Newsome got a restraining order against Bane. If Bane came within a mile of Crystal he would go to jail. Well, Bane, being the hardheaded badass that he is, shrugged off the old man's threat and he and Crystal would sneak around. They did it for years, and then one night when Bane was twenty-two and Crystal not yet eighteen, they eloped."

"Eloped?"

"Yes, but they were found before they could tie the knot." At least that's the story Bane had told them. Riley often wondered if that was the case.

"Anyway," Riley continued, "they returned home and old man Newsome sent Crystal away to live with some relative, and Dillon talked to Bane about getting himself together by making something of himself instead of being a trouble-maker."

Riley paused a moment and then said, "Losing Crystal almost destroyed Bane since he didn't have a clue where she'd gone. Her father made sure of that. We were able to talk Bane into not going after Crystal...at least until he made something of himself and both he and Crystal matured. Bane eventually joined the navy and is working toward being a SEAL."

"Do you think he'll eventually go after Crystal? Find her?"

Riley's frown deepened. "There's no doubt in my mind that he will."

She arched her brow. "You don't seem too happy with the thought of him doing that."

He thought she was very observant. "To be quite honest, I'm not. That whole Crystal thing, with her leaving Denver for parts unknown, nearly destroyed Bane. It's like Crystal is in his blood and he refuses to purge her out of it. She's a part of him that he can't let go of."

He didn't say anything for a long moment. "So yes, Bane will go looking for her one day and he *will* find her. What worries me is the possibility that he will get hurt all over again when he does. For all any of us know, Crystal might have moved on with her life and Bane is just a memory."

As he continued to drive, he decided not to talk anymore for a while. He didn't want anything to ruin his night and thinking of Bane and Crystal would do that for him.

But then maybe he should think about them and, more specifically, recall his brother's agony. Doing so would reinforce the reasons why he would never fall in love with a woman. He refused to ever go through that much pain.

He glanced back over at Alpha. She was quiet, as if she was thinking hard about something. He hoped like hell she wasn't having second thoughts about tonight. He eased out a deep breath when he turned on her street. His overnight bag was in the trunk. When he walked into her house, he intended to stay.

Thoughts of what she and Riley had done back at the restaurant filled Alpha's mind. That had been some dance. She doubted she would ever forget it. While in his arms and connected to him that way, it was as if nothing or no one else existed but the two of them. She'd felt as though the two of them were in their own little world. Never had she done anything so impulsive and spontaneous, so scandalous and wild.

And when they had made love, against the wall of all places, she'd felt sensations take over her body that she'd never felt before. Was this a sample of what she should come to expect from Riley? Anything but the norm? She had a feeling that with him there would never be a dull moment. He had promised her pleasure, and more pleasure, and so far he was right on point.

No man had ever made love to her that way, with such intensity and completeness. And just to think, there was more where that had come from. A lot more.

She blinked when she saw they had arrived at her house already and looked over at Riley when he brought the car to a stop in her driveway. She saw dark, penetrating eyes staring at her. She wondered if there would ever come a day when she would look into his eyes and not get turned on, not feel those incredible sensations flowing through her body.

Without saying anything, he leaned over, unbuckled her seat belt and then reached up and cupped her chin in his hand. "I enjoyed making love to you, Alpha. And I won't apologize for how it happened or where it happened."

She held his gaze. Did he assume the reason she had gotten quiet was because she'd begun having regrets? She held his gaze. "I don't want you to apologize. I asked for it." She chuckled. "You definitely gave me what I wanted, Riley." *What I needed,* she thought.

"Happy to please you, sweetheart."

She didn't have time to think about how easily that term of endearment had rolled off his lips before he was kissing her with an intensity that set her loins on fire. What was there about him that could arouse her so easily, to the point where he had her not only throwing caution to the wind, but also flying in the wind? He had her wanting to try things she'd never thought about doing before.

He slowly ended the kiss, pulled back and stared at her. She felt the intensity of his gaze all the way to the bone. "You had me worried for a minute, when you got quiet on me," he said.

She smiled. "I was merely relishing those moments."

He seemed pleased with what she'd said. "Then let me give you even more of them." He opened the car door and trotted around to her side of the car.

Alpha had a vague memory of him walking her to the front door. And then there was the moment when she'd found it difficult to insert her key into the lock until Riley had eased the key from her nervous hands.

He opened the door and moved aside for her to enter. When she crossed the foyer to the living room, she removed her coat and hung it on the rack before placing her purse on the coffee table. She glanced across the room and saw the fire still kindling in the fireplace, giving the room a warm, toasty feel. She was about to turn to ask Riley if he wanted something to drink when she felt his heat directly behind her. He wrapped his arms around her and pulled her back toward him. Immediately, she felt his aroused body pressed against her backside.

His heated breath touched the side of her face when he whispered, "I want to make love to you in front of the fireplace."

He eased his hold on her so she could turn around in his arms and she stared up into his face. "Sounds like a good plan to me." She leaned forward on tiptoes and slanted her mouth across his.

She wanted to initiate this kiss, master it the best way she knew how, and she figured if she let her tongue do the work that she would be fine. So she kissed him, trying to recall the ways his tongue had driven her crazy. She wanted him to see just how it felt to be on the receiving end this time.

So she feasted on his mouth and he stood there, rock solid, legs braced apart with his arms around her waist, and let her have her way with him. Never had a man's mouth tasted so good. She was enjoying herself so much that she couldn't help moaning in pleasure.

Then, suddenly, she found herself hauled against his hard chest as he took over the kiss, plundering her mouth with his demanding tongue. Desire took over her senses and sent fire through her, blazing hotter than the one in the fireplace.

After that, she couldn't recall how her clothes were removed. The only thing she recalled was being naked while watching in fervent anticipation as he removed his clothes.

When he had taken off the final stitch she couldn't do anything but simply stare. She had seen his erection at the restaurant, but now she was getting a view of the entire picture—the curly strands of dark hair covering his broad chest, rock-hard biceps, lean hips, sinewy thighs and muscled shoulders. But still, her gaze returned to his middle and she couldn't move her eyes away.

She could clearly see that he'd put on a new condom, and when he moved his powerfully built, masculine, naked body toward her, she couldn't help asking, "You do that often?"

"Do what?" he asked coming to a stop directly in front of her, easing his thigh between hers and wrapping his arms around her waist. His action caused her to lose her train of thought for a moment.

He leaned in close, brushed his lips across hers and asked again, "Do what often?"

"Carry a condom with you all the time."

Riley chuckled. "I don't carry one *all* the time, just when I know how the night's going to end. But in some cases, making love might very well be the beginning. I almost lost my head once and messed up and figured I would never come close to letting something like that happen again. It's better to be safe than sorry."

She could arrest his concerns and admit to being on birth control but she knew that with some men it wouldn't matter. They had to have their own form of protection as well, since pregnancy wasn't the only thing a person had to be concerned with.

He leaned in close and nuzzled his nose in her hair. "Mmm, you smell good all over."

His words reclaimed her attention and she lifted her head so she could meet his eyes. "Thanks. So do you."

Riley took a swipe across her lips with his tongue. "You taste good, as well…and I intend to taste you all over, starting now."

Then he claimed her mouth again, just as greedy as before, demolishing any and all of her coherent thoughts. Each and every kiss they shared was more powerful, commanding and potent than the one before it and this one was no different. His mouth ravaged hers, and she couldn't help the moans of pleasure coming from deep within her throat. The man was a great kisser, and he definitely knew how to use that tongue of his.

Being so enmeshed in sharing this heated kiss with Riley, she wasn't aware that they had sunk to their knees in front of the fireplace until he pulled his mouth away and she saw the room beyond his shoulders.

But that observation was short-lived. His mouth left hers to trail kisses along her lips and nibble the sensitive flesh around her mouth. She slid her hand up and down his chest, liking the feel of the curly hair beneath her fingers. She threw her head back when he began sucking her neck then moved slowly down to her shoulder blades. On instinct, she arched backward to rest on her elbows, which caused her breasts to rise upward and her hips to lift off the hearth rug.

His warm breath caressed the side of her face when he whispered, "I love you in this position, and I'm about to show you why."

Riley was convinced he had never wanted any woman this much. Everything about Alpha was perfect, from the smooth slope of her chest, which held two of the most beautiful breasts he'd ever seen, to her firm stomach, curvy hips and thighs and long, shapely legs with gorgeous calves.

Not holding back, he swooped a nipple into his mouth and began sucking on it intensely, hungrily, displaying the voracious sexual appetite that he had for her. With his mouth still clamped to her nipple, he began moving his hand, letting it roam everywhere, but definitely making a path toward the juncture of her thighs. His finger slid inside, finding her not

just wet but drenched. Her hum of pleasure drove him to pen-
etrate deeper and massage her clitoris with circular strokes.

"What are you doing to me, Riley?"

He figured he could ask her the same thing. The womanly
scent emanating from her tempted him to eat her alive. It was
such a luscious, feminine fragrance.

He released her nipple and before moving to latch on to
the other, he glanced up at her and said, "I'm giving you pleasure. I also intend to pay you back for tempting me in the car."

"What did I do?"

"You deliberately flashed me some thigh. Not that I mind.
But it was a hard drive back to your place. No pun intended."

Deciding he didn't want to talk any longer, he began giving her other breast the same ardent attention. He felt her
hand on his head, rubbing gently. And she was shoving her
breast deeper into his mouth. He didn't have a problem with
either movement.

The more he devoured her breasts and inhaled her scent
the more he was thrown into a sexual frenzy. He pulled back,
smiled up at her flushed face, the heavy-lidded eyes staring
back at him. Seeing her so stimulated plunged him into primitive desire, as raw as it could get.

He began licking his way down her body, liking the feel
of his tongue on her skin. And when he dipped his head between her legs and replaced his fingers with his tongue, she
cried out riotously while digging her nails into his back.

He ignored the pain as he lapped her up, using his tongue
to pleasure her the way he'd done in his dreams. He held tight
to her hips when she moved them from side to side, gyrating
against his mouth. He heard her moans, and they were sensual music to his ears.

The trembling of her thighs was the first sign that an explo-
sion was on the horizon, and when she released a deep, throaty
groan followed by a hell-wrenching scream, his tongue pene-

trated deeper within her womanly folds. She pushed her hips upward even more, calling his name.

By the time she lay whimpering softly, he had stretched to settle between her legs. "Alpha?"

She slowly opened her eyes and gazed up at him. A shiver of some unknown force passed through him, gripped him within its clutches. The reflections from the blaze in the fireplace danced across her naked skin, making her even more beautiful. Desirable.

Alpha reached up and cradled his face in her hands. "That was incredible," she whispered.

He wanted to tell her no, that she was incredible. But instead, while still gazing into her eyes, he lifted her hips with his hands and entered her with one smooth thrust.

"Riley!"

"I'm here, baby, and tonight I intend to ride you hard all over the place."

And then he began moving, thrusting within her like the demented sexual maniac that he felt like tonight. The room was filled with the sound of flesh slapping against flesh, moans and groans, and with him whispering words to her that were erotic and wicked.

Then, for the third time that night, he felt her body explode as her inner muscles clenched him hard. He threw his head back and growled her name as he continued to plow her with deep, hard strokes.

He felt his own body shatter and fought to hold it together and couldn't. No orgasm should be this powerful, this mind-blowing, this dominating.

That's the one thing he couldn't let happen. He couldn't let any woman dominate him in any way. He refused to be another Bane. He forced the thought from his mind, deciding no domination would be taking place tonight. He was getting paranoid. He figured over-the-top sex could do that to a man. And this definitely had been over-the-top. She had blasted them off the Richter scale, hands down.

He continued to ride her hard while she wrapped her legs tightly around him. He took her mouth and kissed her with more hunger than he'd ever felt for a woman. His tongue was commanding and demanding as an orgasm continued to rip through him, flinging him to a universe unknown.

The fire roared in the fireplace when a short while later he settled on his back and pulled Alpha into his arms, trying to get their breathing and heartbeats back to normal. He wrapped his arms around her, needing to hold her this way. Not fully understanding why, but just knowing that he did.

She raised her head and looked over at him. "Riley?"

"Hmm?"

She opened her mouth to say something and then, as if she thought better of it, closed her eyes and shook her head. "Nothing."

He lifted a brow. "You sure?"

She nodded. "Yes." She then settled into his arms, snuggling close.

He entwined her legs with his and tightened his hold on her, wondering what she'd been about to say. He glanced down and saw she had dozed off already, breathing gently. Reaching up, he pulled the afghan off the sofa and draped it over their naked bodies.

They would sleep awhile and then wake up and make love some more.

Eleven

"Hey, what did you do this weekend, Alpha? You can barely keep your eyes open. I don't ever recall you being so exhausted."

Alpha took a sip of her coffee as she looked across the table at Lindsey. Her assistant was right; she'd never been this exhausted. But then she'd never had to deal with the likes of Riley Westmoreland before, either.

It had been one heck of a weekend. He hadn't just spent the night with her on Saturday, but had stayed Sunday night, as well. To say it had been wild was an understatement. No matter how many hot baths she'd taken, she couldn't completely work the soreness out of muscles she hadn't used in a long time, if ever. And her hair—for crying out loud, ever since Riley had said he liked it down, that's how she'd worn it. It had been down all weekend, even when it had begun looking tousled and disheveled. When she had mentioned how crazy she must look, he'd said she didn't look crazy, just wildly sexy.

She was convinced Riley had a mental manual in his head

of every sexual position known to mankind and some he probably conjured up himself. He had names for all of them. There had been the Electric Slide, the Ball Game, London Bridge and Sweet Seat, just to name a few. And after kissing her, before leaving this morning, he had assured her with that sexy smile of his that there were plenty more where those had come from.

Needless to say, in one single weekend, the man had given her more orgasms than she'd gotten in her entire life. There had definitely been no climax control. How he stayed up she wasn't sure, but at no time did he go soft on her. He was always forever-ready.

"Alpha," Lindsey said, popping her finger in front of Alpha's face. "Come back down to earth. And why the heavy breathing? Are you all right?"

Alpha set her coffee cup down and smiled at Lindsey. "I'm fine but I admit to feeling tired."

Lindsey scooted back. "You might be coming down with something, so if you don't mind, I'd rather not catch it. With three little ones at home, that would be disastrous."

Alpha nodded, deciding not to tell Lindsey what she had wasn't contagious…unless your bedroom was invaded by the likes of Riley Westmoreland.

Besides, as much as they needed to go over the decorations they'd decided on for the party, she wasn't fully concentrating anyway. "Yes, maybe I need to go back to bed and get some rest after all."

"Sure, but just so you know, I think your decoration ideas are going to wow everyone that night. When do you meet up with Riley Westmoreland again to go over everything?"

Alpha drew in a deep breath. She hadn't a clue. Riley had decided that unless it was a scheduled business meeting, their time together was not about discussing business. Their time was strictly used for pleasure. "I'll probably meet with him in a week or so."

A half hour later Alpha was preparing to take a nap when her phone rang. Her heartbeat kicked up a notch at the thought that the caller might be Riley. She picked up the phone and tried to hide her disappointment when she saw the caller was not Riley, but was, of all people, Eddie. Why was he calling her? It had been more than a year since they had spoken last. She was certain he had gotten on with his life like she had gotten on with hers.

She started not to answer but curiosity had her clicking on the line. "Yes?"

"Alpha, this is Eddie."

"Yes, I know. Your name came up on Caller-ID. This is a surprise."

"Yes. I ran into your father the other day when I took Cleo in."

"Okay."

"I asked your dad about you. I'd heard you moved to Colorado."

"Yes, I'm living in Denver. I love it here."

He chuckled. "But I'm sure you hate the weather. You and I both know you don't like anything cold."

He was right. So why had she tolerated *him* for so long? It had taken spending time with Riley to realize Eddie had been as cold as a dead fish. "Yes, well, sometimes we learn to tolerate things that aren't good for us."

He didn't say anything for a moment and then, "I'll be in Denver on business next week and I'd like to see you while I'm out there."

She lifted a brow. "Why? Nothing has changed, Eddie. I didn't go along with your ultimatum, and there was nothing left to be said."

"I'm beginning to think that's not the case."

Not the case? She held the phone away from her ear and stared at it. Was she really talking to Eddie? The man who hadn't hesitated to dump her a week before their wedding because she wouldn't let him control her? "Well, I know that *is* the case. You made your decision."

"Yes, but since you and your twin aren't on speaking terms…"

Not on speaking terms? Where in the world did he get such erroneous information? "That's not true. Omega and I are closer than ever. Where did you hear such a ridiculous thing?"

He didn't say anything for a minute. "From your father. And even if it isn't true, I think that it should be."

Anger flared up within her when she heard the sharpness in his voice. "And what if I told you that I don't give a royal damn what you think? Now, goodbye and please don't bother calling me again."

She hung up the phone, furious with herself for answering Eddie's call in the first place. He hadn't changed. He still expected her to adhere to his wishes like a good little girl. The man just didn't get it.

As she crawled on top of the bed for her nap, she couldn't help but recall that the last time she'd been in it, Riley had been with her. Shifting, she pushed a wayward curl from her face as she lay on her side with her head resting on her hands, wondering how long it would take for the soreness to work itself out of her body. When she picked up Riley's scent, which was entrenched on the pillow, she closed her eyes, remembering the weekend. As desire gripped her… of all places…between her sore legs, she knew she couldn't wait to see him again.

After his meeting, Riley made it back to his office with both Canyon and Stern on his heels. He went straight to his desk, sat down and sent both brothers a questioning look. They were standing in the middle of his office with smirks on their faces.

"Okay, what's going on with you two?" he asked.

Stern crossed his arms over his chest and chuckled. "We

should be asking you what's going on. You could barely keep your eyes open during that meeting with Dillon. We expected him to call you out for dozing."

Riley rubbed a frustrated hand down his face. Had he really dozed off in one of Dillon's meetings? Especially one that Dillon had specifically come into the office to hold with them?

"You must have had one hell of a weekend, Ry," Canyon said, eyeing him curiously. "I dropped by Riley's Station a couple of times and it was apparent you weren't home. That means you were gone *all* weekend. Must be some hot number you're seeing."

Straightening in his seat, Riley picked up a file off his desk. Instead of responding to Canyon's comment, he said, "Don't you guys have other things to do? Because if you don't, I do."

"Will you be able to stay awake long enough to do any work?" Stern asked, grinning.

He was about to tell his brother where he could go…in not-so-nice words…when there was a quick knock at the door just before Dillon walked in. He smiled when he saw his three brothers. "Good, all three of you are here. I just got a call from Mack Owens. He's ready to sell that piece of land we've had our eyes on for a strip mall in Memphis. The trip will last until Sunday since Mack and his wife are hosting a dinner party Saturday night. Which one of you wants to go and close the deal with Mack?"

Riley could see both Stern and Canyon easing toward the door. Evidently they had hot dates for the weekend. But then so did he. He had invited Alpha to the movies Saturday night. He was about to tell Dillon he had plans but quickly changed his mind. Dillon was depending on them to keep things running smoothly while he was away from the office. And if Canyon and Stern had other plans that meant things fell on his shoulders. Going to Tennessee wouldn't be so bad if he could talk Alpha into going with him.

"I'll be able to go to Memphis, Dil. When do you need me to leave?"

"Thursday, if possible."

Riley nodded. "Okay, I don't see a problem." He glanced over at Canyon and Stern and took note of their relieved expressions. They owed him big-time.

"Good." Dillon headed for the door but then suddenly turned back around. "You're evidently keeping late hours someplace, Ry. I suggest that you get some rest."

Ignoring the "we told you so" grins on Stern's and Canyon's faces, he said, "I will."

When Dillon left, Riley glared at his brothers. "The only reason I decided to go to Tennessee is because the two of you evidently had important plans for this weekend."

Canyon waved off his words. "We do, and we appreciate you being the sacrificial lamb this time. Mack Owens has a tendency to bore you to tears."

"Whatever. Now will the two of you leave so I can get some work done?"

Moments later, after his brothers had cleared out of his office, Riley leaned back in his chair, finding it hard to believe he'd actually dozed off during one of Dillon's meetings. There was no excuse for that. However, he would be the first to admit he'd experienced one hell of a weekend. It had been simply incredible. He closed his eyes as erotic memories flowed through his mind.

First, he and Alpha had made love in front of the fireplace, then when they'd gotten hungry they went into the kitchen for a snack and ended up making love in there, as well. He had introduced her to the Courting Chair position. Never before had he enjoyed making love to a woman who was not only open to trying different things but was as exciting, energetic and beautiful as any woman could be.

He reached for the phone, but then hung it up before the first ring. He would wait until later tonight to call her when he could be assured there would not be any interruptions.

He opened the file in the middle of his desk, hoping that Alpha would agree to go with him to Tennessee. If she did, he would certainly make the trip worth her while. He would guarantee it.

Later that night, Alpha sat on the sofa going through her book of party favors. Since this would be the fortieth anniversary of Blue Ridge, the Westmorelands wanted each attendee to leave with a favor that would remind them not only of the significance of that night, but also of the party theme. She had marked a few items she thought would be perfect and still within the budget. The vendors she'd spoken with had pretty much guaranteed everything would arrive well in advance of the party date.

A log broke in the fireplace and the pop made her look up. It was then that she remembered making love to Riley, right there in front of the fireplace on the hearth rug. It had been simply amazing, and the memory caused flutters in her stomach. But then, she thought, every time they'd made love had been off the charts.

She stood and stretched, feeling well rested after her nap. She wasn't as sore as she'd been that morning, which she thought was a good thing. Tomorrow she had an eleven o'clock appointment with the granddaughter of a couple who would be celebrating their seventieth wedding anniversary on Valentine's Day. And on Wednesday she would be meeting with a woman who was giving herself a fiftieth birthday party in April.

Omega had called a few hours ago, wanting to know everything about her weekend with Riley. Of course Alpha hadn't told her sister every little detail, but she'd shared enough for Omega to draw her own conclusions about how well her weekend had gone. She hadn't mentioned Eddie's call, since she didn't want to upset her sister. But Alpha intended to talk to her father, who apparently had encouraged Eddie's call.

She was about to head to the kitchen for a cup of hot chocolate when her cell phone rang. She leaned down to pick it up off the table. "Hello."

"You've really done it this time, Alpha. The only reason Eddie called you was because I talked to him that day and told him you would love hearing from him."

Alpha drew in a deep breath upon hearing her father's voice. "You had no right to tell him Omega and I weren't speaking when you know that is not true, Dad. Things are over between Eddie and me. Why can't you accept that?"

"He'd take you back if you got your act together and did what he's asking. You shouldn't let your sister come between you and the man you love."

Alpha gritted her teeth, trying to hold back from telling her father just how wrong and unfair he was, and had always been, to his other child.

"I'll let you go so you can think about it, Al." She then heard a click in her ear. She shook her head. Not for the first time, her father had hung up on her.

Her phone rang. And not for the first time he would call her right back to give her more of an earful, but she had news for him. She clicked on the phone. "Listen, Dad. No matter what you want, Eddie and I are not getting back together. I'm seeing someone else now, and he's more of a man than Eddie will ever be."

There was a moment of silence and then a deep, husky voice said, "I'm glad you think so."

Alpha closed her eyes. *Ah, hell.*

"Alpha?"

She had gotten quiet on him, Riley thought. He didn't know what had prompted her to pick up the phone and say what she had, but evidently she and her father had been having quite an interesting conversation before he'd called. And evidently her father was a huge supporter of her ex-fiancé.

"Yes?"

"Are you okay?" he asked with concern in his voice.

"Yes. Sorry about that. I thought you were my father calling back."

"I see." He waited to see if she would expound on that. Instead, she changed the subject by saying, "I'm surprised you called. I hadn't expected to hear from you until the weekend."

"Yes, that had been my plan but something has come up. I'll be leaving town on Thursday for Memphis and won't be back until Sunday."

"Oh."

Was that disappointment he heard in her voice? "I was calling to let you know and to see if you wanted to go to Memphis with me."

There was a pause and then, "You want me to go out of town with you?"

"Yes. I have a meeting Friday morning and will be attending a social event Saturday night. I'd like you to be there with me. However, if you can't clear your calendar on such short notice, I understand."

"No, I'd love to go."

Riley released a breath he'd just realized he'd been holding. "That's great. We'll fly out around noon on Thursday. Have you ever been to Memphis before?"

"No."

"Then I'm going to enjoy showing you around. I've been there a number of times."

"Sounds like fun. I look forward to going."

There was another reason he had called. One that had concerned him since leaving her. "Are you okay? When I left you this morning you were quite sore." He, of all people, had been aware of the intensity of their lovemaking, but it was as if they hadn't been able to get enough of each other.

"Yes, I'm fine."

"Good." For some reason, he wasn't ready to end the call yet. "So what did you do today?"

He listened as she talked, liking the way she sounded. He had come home, showered and was sitting in his living room on the sofa with his legs stretched out in front of him, alone in the dark, talking to her. He had stopped by his brother Jason's place for dinner, and had enjoyed the time he spent with Jason's wife, Bella, and the twins.

"I'm glad you were able to take a long nap," he said, wishing he could have been there to take the nap with her. He had ended up leaving the office earlier than usual to go to the gym. It had taken a good workout to get his adrenaline flowing again. And talking to her now was a definite boost. There was nothing else he'd rather be doing. *Monday Night Football* couldn't even compete.

They talked for a while longer, and she did sneak in information about the favors she'd come across that she thought would be perfect for the party. They continued talking about some of everything, including which NFL team they thought would make it to the Super Bowl.

All too soon he glanced at the clock on the table and saw it was after midnight. "Sorry," he said, standing to stretch.

"What are you apologizing for?"

"For the third night straight I've kept you up late." He was certain he didn't have to remind her of what they'd been doing those other two nights around this time.

"No apology needed, Riley."

He liked the way she'd said his name just now. He liked it even better when she screamed it in the middle of an orgasm. And she'd done that a lot over the weekend. "Well, I'm not going to keep you. I enjoyed talking to you tonight. And I'm looking forward to our trip to Memphis."

"I enjoyed talking to you as well and can't wait until we leave on Thursday."

By the time he had ended the call, Riley knew the one thing was happening that he hadn't intended to happen.

Alpha Blake was getting under his skin.

Twelve

"Welcome to the Peabody, Mr. and Mrs. Westmoreland."

Alpha tried to keep a straight face when she heard the hotel clerk's erroneous assumption. She glanced over at Riley, who was standing beside her, and wondered if he would correct the man. He didn't. Instead, he smiled and winked at her.

"Thank you," he said, accepting the passkey.

"I hope your stay here is a great one," the man added.

"I'm sure that it will be."

Taking Alpha's hand in his, Riley led her to the bank of elevators. As they waited, he leaned in close and whispered, "He made an honest mistake."

She nodded, not saying anything because she didn't see how the man could have made that mistake when neither she nor Riley had rings on their fingers. When the elevator arrived, they stepped inside along with several others. Every aspect of the hotel was gorgeous, even right down to the spacious and elegantly designed elevator car. She tried concentrating on the small television screen mounted above the door. Everyone's attention was glued to the commentary. Everyone's except hers and Riley's.

Their attention was on each other and had been since he'd picked her up to take her to the airport. He'd carried her luggage out to his truck, but not before kissing her in a way that had made her panties wet.

Now, the elevator stopped on the fifth floor and she moved aside to let a couple off. She immediately felt the warm rush of blood that flowed through her veins when Riley placed his arms around her waist and pulled her closer to his side.

When the elevator reached their floor, he led her out. Holding her hand, he walked beside her down the beautifully decorated corridor to their room. Although there hadn't been a discussion about it, she and Riley would be sharing a room. She hadn't thought of staying anywhere else.

They came to a stop and Riley let go of her hand to open the door. With an efficiency she wasn't surprised he had, he opened the door and then stood aside for her to enter.

She walked into the room and looked around. It was a beautiful suite, almost as large as her home. She was about to tell Riley just how beautiful the room was when strong arms encircled her waist and turned her around.

The eyes staring down at her were so full of need and desire that it sent a sensuous shudder through her. It didn't take much to recall all they'd done the last time they were together. A replay of those vivid erotic images had done a number on her mind all week.

"I missed you this week," he said huskily.

She couldn't help the smile that touched her lips. It was nice knowing she was missed. She had definitely missed him, as well. "You know where I live," she said teasingly.

He chuckled softly. "Yes, and trust me, not paying you a visit was one of the hardest things I've ever done. But your body needed a time-out. It had quite a workout last weekend."

"Now that's an understatement," she said, her smile widening.

He didn't say anything and she could have sworn she saw a guarded look in his eyes, but then he leaned in closer and asked, "Have I told you how much I like you?"

"No, I don't believe you have."

"Well, let me go on record by saying, I like you, Alpha Blake. Probably more so than I should."

She was about to ask what he meant by that when he quickly said, "Come on, we need to get out of this room. Let's do dinner and then a night of blues on Beale Street."

A few hours later, while walking down Beale Street, Riley couldn't help glancing over at the woman walking beside him, the woman whose hand was firmly held in his. When was the last time he and any woman had walked down a street holding hands?

Never.

So why was he doing so now? Sex with no commitment was just what it sounded like. No strings attached. No reason to lie and promise the moon, the stars or the sky. And no drama, since he'd laid out the rules. Why weren't they up in the hotel room making out since that's all their relationship was supposed to be?

He drew in a deep breath. And when was the last time he'd gone barhopping? Yet here he was, strolling down Beale Street, going from club to club, bar to bar, while holding hands with a woman he'd confessed to liking.

But what really riled him up was that he'd gotten angry when he'd seen a couple of guys checking her out at one of the clubs. He would be the first to admit she looked damn good in her jeans, but still. Why had he gotten jealous? It wasn't as if he had a serious relationship going on with Alpha. She was merely his sex partner for six weeks.

"This place is wonderful," she said, breaking into his

thoughts. Excitement and gaiety shone in her eyes. "I've really never appreciated the blues until now. Thanks."

His hand tightened around hers. "I should be thanking you. If you weren't here I would be up in my hotel room on my laptop getting a start on next week's work. You've turned what probably would have been a boring trip into a fun one."

She threw her head back and laughed before arching a perfect brow. "Truly you don't want me to believe that Riley Westmoreland would not have had fun without me?"

Yes, he wanted her to believe it because it was true. Yes, he would have had some degree of fun, but not like this. They had enjoyed some fabulous foods, had taken over the dance floor a few times and he'd even talked her into karaoke, a Billie Holiday number.

He stopped walking, reached out and lifted her chin with his fingertip. "I never say anything I don't mean, Alpha, and this is the most fun I've ever had with any woman."

She slid her hand up over his chest. "I'm glad."

He was tempted to kiss her but held back. There would be plenty of time for kisses when he got her back to their hotel room. Tightening her hand in his once more, he began walking again.

He glanced over at her. "So what are your plans tomorrow while I'm in my meetings?"

She leaned up on tiptoe, nuzzled her nose in the side of his face and whispered, "Depends on how well you wear me out tonight. If I'm up to it, I plan to go shopping. Christmas is next month, you know."

Yes, he knew, and they would have ended their affair by then. "You got a lot of people to buy for?" he asked.

"Umm, just the usual."

She was being evasive again. "You plan on going home for Christmas or staying in Denver?"

"Haven't decided yet."

"Does your family get together for the holidays?" he asked

her, holding tight to her hand and looking both ways before they crossed the street.

"No, not everyone." Then, as if she wanted to get a question of her own in, she quickly asked, "What about with your family? Will everyone be home for Christmas?"

"This Christmas, yes, mainly because of the holiday party, with it being the fortieth anniversary and all. I believe our parents, aunt and uncle would have wanted us all together, celebrating something that major. Bane won't be able to make it since he's on assignment someplace, but Gemma and her family are coming from Australia."

"Sounds like the Westmorelands will be having a fun time. And as the event planner for the holiday party, I intend to make it a night to remember." She smiled over at him.

He returned her smile. "I believe it." And he did. On the plane, she had gone over her decorating ideas with him and he could tell she was a person who was on top of every single detail.

"So what about it?"

He blinked, aware that Alpha had asked him something. "Sorry, what did you say?"

She smiled and the warmth of that smile filled him with something he couldn't name. She leaned closer to him. "I suggested that we call it a night and head back to our hotel. Are you okay with that?"

Instead of answering her, he stepped off the sidewalk and pulled her into the shadows where two buildings connected. They could still partially be seen but he didn't care. He pulled her body to his, lowered his mouth and kissed her—long, hard and deep, tangling his tongue with hers.

Moments later, he released her mouth and pressed his forehead to hers. "Did you get the answer you wanted just now?" he asked slowly, trying to catch his breath.

He felt the curve of her smile against his lips. "Most definitely."

* * *

There was no doubt in Alpha's mind, as she watched a naked Riley stride out of the bathroom, that he was what any woman would consider a hottie of mega proportions. And speaking of proportions… Her gaze lowered to his middle. He was aroused and had already sheathed his thick erection in a condom. Her gaze stayed glued to that part of him as he approached the bed.

He caressed the side of her face with his finger.

"Why are you staring at me like that? You don't think what I'm packing is real?"

She looked up at him. "Oh, I know it's real. I'm just wondering how it tastes."

She saw the flash of intense desire fill his eyes, making them dark orbs of heated lust and her heart started racing wildly. She'd never been so bold with a man before. It was almost unbelievable how comfortable she felt with Riley, to the point where she would say just about anything.

He held her gaze and then said in a low tone, "Then I guess I'll let you find out."

He moved his hand from her face, and she watched as he slowly, methodically, removed the condom and dropped it in the wastepaper basket near the bed. He then looked at her. "Now what do you want me to do?" he asked.

She scooted over in the huge bed and patted a spot. "I want you here. On your back."

The bed dipped beneath his weight as he joined her, lying flat on his back as she'd instructed. She then eased between his thighs, lifting them up so his knees braced both sides of her head. On her knees, she smiled down at him. "I'm sure there's a name for this position already, right?"

He swallowed deeply before nodding. "Heels Over Head."

Alpha nodded. "Sounds appropriate." She then eased her head down to his aroused shaft. He was huge. Gigantic. And the veins running along the engorged head were so easily visible that she swore she could see the blood rushing through them.

She touched him and appreciated the solid weight she held in her hand. He was so large it took both hands to hold him— definitely a handful—and she figured that he would be a mouthful, as well. She was about to find out.

Alpha opened her mouth over the head of his penis and her tongue swiped across it before fully taking him in. And once her lips locked down on him, she went to work, licking every inch of him, loving his taste. His masculine moans of sexual gratification made her feel totally feminine.

He gripped several locks of her hair but she felt no pain, only pleasure. He had a unique way of educating her and satisfying her needs at the same time. Describing what he would be doing to her in vivid detail was just as arousing as him actually doing it.

That was one of the reasons she wanted to make this special for him. He probably could tell she was a novice, but hopefully he would see that at least her heart was in it. And the thought that his heavy shaft was fully lodged in her mouth was a total turn-on for her. From the sounds he was making, he apparently liked everything she was doing. Encouraged by his response, she closed her eyes and turned up the heat, intent on satisfying her man.

Her man?

Where had that thought come from? But instead of dismissing it totally, she accepted that for all of six weeks, he would be her man. And then on the night of the holiday party, her fantasy fling would come to an end.

"Alpha…"

Her name, growled from deep within his throat, filled her with intense desire. She knew every long lick of her tongue, and the deep suction she was applying, was sending him over the edge just the way she wanted.

She opened her eyes when she felt a hard tug on her hair,

as he tried to get her mouth off him, but she held tight. He finally gave up and let go. She tasted the essence of him as he filled her mouth.

Moments later she released him and before she could say how tasty he was, he rolled over, pulled her down to her stomach and straddled her back. With his legs tucked between hers, he lifted her hips. In one smooth thrust, he entered her, going as deep as he could. He then leaned down close and whispered against the back of her neck, "This is called Inside Out."

She soon found out why when he began thrusting in and out of her hard, extending as far as her womb and then back again. She felt him in every stroke, and it was only then that she realized he wasn't wearing a condom.

"Riley, the condom!"

He went still. But she didn't. At least not on the inside where her muscles continued to clench him, milking him hard. His deep growl sent sensations through her pelvis, electrifying her spine. She expected him to pull out immediately but instead he leaned down so close that she felt his heated breath against her ear. "Please tell me you're on the pill or something, baby."

His plea was tortured and she was more than happy to erase his concerns. "Yes, I'm on the pill."

As if that was what he needed to hear, he began moving again, with even more urgency than before, stroking her deeply, growling like a primitive animal performing his last mating ritual. She felt him in every muscle of her body and shivers of pleasure rammed up and down her spine with every hard thrust. Then she felt him explode deep in her womb. His hand cupped tight to her bare bottom, tilted it at an angle that hit a spot that sent her screaming. She buried her head in the pillow to smother the sound, but it did nothing to the sensations ripping her apart. On top of everything, she felt his mouth on her back, nibbling her skin, licking it, nibbling some more. Branding her.

"Riley!"

Her body began quaking, all the way to her toes. Sensations overtook her. Pure feminine satisfaction tore through her, and she shivered with an intensity that shook the entire bed as pent-up passion was released from deep within her. When she collapsed, totally drained, he flipped her on her back and lifted her hips. Using the missionary position, he reentered her. She looked up at him, amazed, although, if the truth be known, she shouldn't be astonished. She had found out last weekend that Riley Westmoreland had the stamina of a bull.

And although she didn't think it was possible, a moment later he brought them both to yet another orgasm, and she knew this was only the beginning.

There would definitely be no climax control tonight.

Thirteen

"I'm glad you're going to be my wedding planner, Alpha."

"And I'm glad you chose me for the job."

Alpha sipped her tea as she studied Megan Westmoreland—Megan Claiborne in six months. She thought Megan, who was a doctor of anesthesiology at one of the local hospitals, was a beautiful woman. And Alpha could see the Westmoreland similarities in the dark eyes, perfectly arched brows and cheekbones.

Other than Dillon and his wife, Pam, Alpha hadn't met any other family members. Due to the nature of her and Riley's relationship, there was no need for him to introduce her to his family and she was certain that none of them were aware they were having an affair.

Alpha's thoughts shifted back to the bride-to-be. Megan's engagement party had been held earlier in the month. With that out of the way, Megan was ready to plan her June wedding. Alpha had gotten the call on Monday, the day she had returned to Denver from spending four wonderful days in

Memphis with Riley. Goose bumps formed on her arms whenever she thought about just how fantastic those days had been.

"So you like the wedding colors I've selected?" Megan asked.

Alpha's attention was pulled back to the business at hand. "Yes, I think buttercup and lime are wonderful colors together. They give me a lot to work with."

Megan seemed pleased with that. "I'm glad."

They were in the middle of discussing the food items Megan wanted as part of her menu when Megan's front door opened and a man, who Alpha knew immediately had to be one of Riley's brothers or cousins, stalked in with a furious expression on his face.

A calm Megan glanced over at him and asked, "What has you so riled this morning, Zane?"

So this was Zane Westmoreland? Alpha thought, sipping her tea, trying not to let it be so obvious that she was checking him out. Since arriving in town, she'd heard a lot of feminine whispers about him. Women thought he was hot and she could see why. But then, Riley was hot, as well. Even hotter, in her book. But she would be the first to admit she was biased where Riley was concerned.

"This is Alpha Blake. She's helping me plan my wedding," Megan added, introducing them.

The man gave a quick tip of his Stetson in Alpha's direction before returning his full attention to Megan. "What's this I hear about Channing Hastings being on your invitation list?"

Megan smiled sweetly. "Yes, what of it?"

"I don't want her at your wedding."

Megan put her teacup down and gave her brother her full attention. "Why? No matter how your relationship with Channing ended, if you recall, she and I worked together at the hospital long before the two of you met. I've always liked her and still consider her a friend and—"

"I don't want her there, Megan."

Megan frowned. "It's my wedding, Zane, and she's invited, so if you have to get yourself together before seeing her again then I suggest—"

"That's not it," he snapped.

"Sounds like it is," Megan countered.

Instead of saying anything else, Zane Westmoreland turned and stormed out the door with the same turbulent gust of wind that had brought him in. When the door slammed shut behind him, Megan glanced over at Alpha with an apologetic smile on her face. "As you can see, not all the Westmorelands are civilized."

Alpha took another sip of her tea before asking, "Are you sure you don't want me to remove Ms. Hastings's name from the invitation list?"

Megan smiled. "I'm positive. It's time my brother comes to terms with his true feelings about some things."

An hour later, Alpha had wrapped up her meeting with Megan and stood, ready to go, when there was a knock at Megan's door. Alpha wondered if Zane had calmed down and was returning.

"Come in," Megan called out.

The door opened and Alpha's heart almost fell from her chest when Riley walked in.

Megan glanced over at her cousin. "Riley, if you're here on Zane's behalf to talk me out of inviting Channing to the—"

"No," he interrupted. "Channing is Zane's issue. He has to deal with it. You have the right to invite who you want."

His gaze shifted from Megan to Alpha. "But he did mention you had company, your wedding planner, so I thought I'd drop by to say hello."

Megan looked curiously from Alpha to Riley. "You two have met already?"

Riley nodded. "Yes, I'm working with Alpha on the holiday party at Blue Ridge next month."

Megan tapped her forehead. "That's right. How could I

forget you're coordinating that? Last time I heard you were doing it grudgingly, Riley. Evidently that has changed."

Megan would be surprised to learn just how much things had changed, Riley thought. "Yes, that has changed."

Megan smiled. "I'm glad to hear it."

When Riley didn't say anything but continued to look at Alpha, in a way that probably seemed like he could eat her alive, Megan cleared her throat. "Is that the only reason you dropped by?" she asked.

He shifted his gaze from Alpha back to Megan. "Not really. I wanted to ask Alpha something."

He glanced over at Alpha again. "My family is doing their monthly out-on-the-town dinner Wednesday night at Mc-Kay's. I wanted to know if you'd like to come? That way you can meet the rest of the family. I think they'd like to get acquainted with the person putting the party together."

Out of the corner of his eye, he saw Megan raise a brow, because in truth, there was no need for the family to get to know the person putting the party together. He knew it and she knew it, as well.

Luckily Alpha didn't know it. She smiled and said, "Yes, I'm available Wednesday night to meet the rest of your family."

"Good. I'll pick you up at six."

He glanced over at Megan, who was still staring at him. She was probably wondering why he offered to pick up Alpha when anyone living in Denver clearly knew the directions to McKay's.

"That will be fine and I'll be ready," Alpha said.

He began backing out of the house before Megan felt the need to ask him anything. "Great, I'll see you again later, then." And he meant that literally because he planned to drop by her place tonight.

"All right."

He turned and headed to the door in quick, powerful

strides. She'd looked good in her dark brown slacks and peach-colored pullover sweater. The coloring was perfect for her complexion. And her hair was loose and fanned around her shoulders, just the way he liked.

He told himself to keep walking to the door, to open it and not look back. But for some reason, he couldn't do that. When he opened the door and glanced back over his shoulder, he looked directly at Alpha. She was holding his gaze and he felt that sensual chemistry that had his body tingling with the same powerful awareness he felt whenever he was around her. He smiled at Alpha and she smiled back.

There was no way his perceptive cousin hadn't picked up on the exchange, which was probably the reason she kept looking back and forth between him and Alpha. She would have questions, he didn't doubt that, but he would deal with his cousin's nosiness later.

"Ry?"

He switched his gaze from Alpha to Megan, aware that Megan had said something. "Yes?"

"Either come in or go out. Holding the door open is letting out the heat," she said with an amused expression on her face.

"Oh. Okay, I'm leaving." He firmly closed the door behind him.

Riley smiled as he headed for his truck, but once he got inside, buckled his seat belt and saw his reflection in his rearview mirror, he frowned. What the hell was wrong with him? As soon as an angry Zane mentioned Alpha was at Megan's, he hadn't wasted time getting over there, leaving Zane staring at him like he'd lost his mind.

And, in a way, he was afraid that he had.

The first of the craziness had been making love to Alpha without a condom. Since the first time he'd made out with Emily Parker at the age of fourteen, he'd always used a condom. His father had had "the talk" with all his sons when they turned thirteen, and Dillon had reinforced those talks over the years. Since no form of birth control was 100 percent, it hadn't mattered one iota if the woman claimed to be on the pill or any other kind of birth control. His rule was to use a condom.

Why had he broken that rule for Alpha?

Granted, being inside her—skin-to-skin, flesh-to-flesh, feeling the way her inner muscles had clamped on him—had felt out of this world. Totally awesome. Even so, there was no reason for him to take chances, and he'd continued to take chances. He hadn't used a condom with her since they'd arrived back in Denver yesterday morning.

He leaned back in his seat. It didn't take much to remember the four days he and Alpha had spent together in Memphis. Words couldn't describe how much he had enjoyed the trip, and it had nothing to do with him signing off on that business deal. It had everything to do with Alpha being in Memphis with him.

He had finalized the contract early and had returned to the hotel room to find she'd gone shopping. He had paced the floor like an obsessed man, and the moment she had returned, he had swept her into his arms, making all her shopping bags go flying.

He'd never known he could undress a woman so quickly. Within moments they were both naked and back in the bed again. Saturday, they had done a tour of the city, including Graceland and the hotel where Martin Luther King Jr. had lost his life.

Then on Saturday night they had gone to Mack's dinner party. She had looked fantastic, and he'd known she would wow everyone just like she'd wowed him. He'd actually regretted packing up and leaving Memphis yesterday.

Drawing in a deep breath, he straightened and started the ignition. Now he'd done the unthinkable and invited her to share dinner with his family. He could just imagine what all of them would think when he arrived at McKay's with Alpha on Wednesday night.

He was beginning to act real crazy with her. That wasn't a good thing.

The best thing to do would be to put distance between them until the family dinner.

The last person Alpha expected to see when she opened her door later that evening was Riley. "Riley," she said, moving aside to let him come in. "I was just about to grab something to eat. Do you want to join me?"

"I'd love to."

She closed the door behind him. "You're not going to ask what's for dinner?"

"Doesn't matter. I came to see you. Dinner is an extra."

He'd come to see her, and she didn't have to guess why. The man had a ferocious sexual appetite that was contagious. But she had no complaints. He'd unleashed something within her. She would admit that she wanted him as much as he wanted her.

"And, if you're in the mood, after dinner I thought we'd grab a movie."

She glanced over at him. "A movie?"

"Yes."

"I'd love to but…"

He raised a brow. "But what?"

"I've already made plans for the evening."

"Oh," he said, and she could tell by his expression that he was surprised. "I apologize. I should have called first."

"No reason for you to do that. I figured it was time for me to organize my junk room and planned to spend the evening doing just that."

"Your junk room?"

She smiled. "Yes. Whenever I'm out and about and see anything that captures my interest, anything I feel just might work for a future party theme, I bring it home and stick it in my junk room. Needless to say, the room is pretty disorganized now."

He chuckled. "Need my help?"

She was surprised by his offer. "You want to help?"

"Yes."

She thought of all the other things he could be doing tonight. "Are you sure you want to do that?"

"Positive. Besides, it's the least I can do to thank you for inviting me to dine with you."

Alpha waved off his words with her hand. "No need to thank me. And if you're sure about helping, then thanks. I can certainly use it. It's been a while since I got things organized in that room, and I was determined that tonight would be when I started on it."

"Then count me in."

"Every time I eat a meal you prepare, I'm impressed," Riley said, leaning back in the chair as he used a napkin to wipe the corners of his mouth.

"You've only eaten two meals prepared by me," Alpha said, grinning.

"Then I've been impressed twice."

She threw her head back and laughed. He loved the sound. It was rich, feminine and genuine. It didn't matter at that moment that earlier that day he'd sworn to put distance between them. All it took was him being home alone with a deep craving to see her again. It was a craving that had him taking a shower, changing clothes and driving over to see her like a demented fool.

They sat and talked about her plans for Megan's wedding and then he helped her clear the table before assisting her in loading the dishes in the dishwasher. For no reason, other than he wanted to kiss her, he took her hand and pulled her to him. The feel of her hardened nipples pressing against his chest made him draw in a deep breath and fill his nostrils with her scent.

"I need to kiss you," he whispered against her lips before leaning in closer and claiming them. He maneuvered his arms around her waist to bring her closer to him. He enjoyed being inside her mouth, licking her from corner to corner, tasting her deeply as their tongues tangled passionately. And he definitely loved the sounds she made, those sensual moans of pleasure that made his mouth even hungrier for hers. He could lock lips with her for hours, days, weeks…well past six weeks.

He broke off the kiss but continued to hold her in his arms while inwardly chastising himself for even thinking such a thing. He would admit it was a novelty to want a woman this much, but he would eventually get over it. However, he would be the first to admit she wasn't making it easy. When she peered up at him, it was the most natural thing to brush his lips across hers.

A number of other women had been eager to say or do whatever was needed in the hope that he would extend his six-week rule. It hadn't happened. Yet he knew he would make Alpha the exception, if she was interested. But he had a feeling she wasn't. Why did it bother him that she wasn't interested in going beyond the six weeks like the others?

"Hey, don't think a few kisses will get you out of helping me," she said, placing her hands on his shoulders.

Tempted, and giving in to it, he leaned down again to trace a kiss along the nape of her neck. "Let me assure you, I'm not trying to get out of anything. Although I'll admit a few naughty thoughts have crossed my mind."

"There's always later," she whispered.

He wondered if she knew how much that promise made his erection throb. He went back to her lips, loving the feel of how they quivered beneath his. "Actually, I was hoping…"

She threw her head back. "Now, why doesn't that surprise me?" She took a step back. "Come on and let's tackle that room before we're tempted to get into something else."

He followed her from the kitchen to where her bedrooms were located. She passed her sleeping quarters and opened the door of another room.

He walked in behind her and glanced around. He'd seen junkier rooms, but her collection of items intrigued him. He walked across the room and picked up the For Sale sign and looked back at her. "Moving?"

She shook her head and smiled. "No, I kept that because you never know when I might have a moving party for someone."

He nodded and picked up another item. "Boxing gloves?"

She shrugged. "You never know when they might come in handy, as well, for one of my future events."

He picked up several other items, and she provided her reasons for grabbing them either from a store or a yard sale. "Okay, Ms. Blake. Tell me what we need to do to get this show on the road."

She rubbed her hands together as he rolled up his sleeves. "Okay. I've already named those huge plastic tubs over there by traditional party themes—birthday, wedding, anniversary, retirement and new baby. All we have to do is put them in the designated tub."

That sounded easy enough. "And if I'm not sure which one will fit?"

"Then remember the name of my business, Imagine, and let your imagination go to work. If you're still in doubt, then just drop it in the miscellaneous tub for me to sort through later."

"Okay."

He quickly went to work, knowing what was on the agenda for later. She had turned on a radio and, except for the music floating around the room, the only other sounds were those they made moving around while putting items in order. Using his imagination like she'd said, he put every item he picked up into what he felt was the appropriate tub. He tossed a few items in the miscellaneous tub when, for the life of him, he could not figure out what she'd had in mind when she'd bought it.

He thought they worked well together and within an hour he could definitely see them making progress. He glanced over at her. She had removed her pullover sweater to uncover a T-shirt that said Look at Me and Imagine. He smiled, thinking he could definitely do that.

At that moment, he could imagine her without a stitch of clothing, spread on top of the table where they'd eaten earlier. He could see her long legs dangling off the sides as he stepped between them after removing all his own clothes. He could further imagine taking his favorite jam—strawberry—and smearing it all over her body, then taking his time licking it off. He could imagine the tip of his tongue covering every inch of her and—

"Taking an unscheduled break, Riley?"

Her voice sliced into his daydream. He blinked, realizing he had been standing there staring at her, for no telling how long. Swearing under his breath, he shook his head. "No, I was just checking out your T-shirt."

"My T-shirt?" she asked, looking down at herself with a quizzical expression on her face. "Oh," she said, in a tone that let him know she'd forgotten about what was written on her shirt.

He couldn't hold back the smile that crept into his features. "Nice."

She shrugged. "It was a gift from my sister and meant to be funny."

He hadn't seen anything amusing about it. It had the opposite effect. Those had been some serious musings stirring his imagination. Pretty damn hot musings, in fact. "Really?"

"Yes, sometimes she has a warped sense of humor."

He would take her word for it since he'd noticed how she would change the subject when any discussion of her family came up. "Well, I think it's nice, and it's time to get back to work. We're almost finished."

She nodded and went back to folding up tablecloths of just about every color you could name. He latched his attention onto one of the last items he needed to put away, one of those bouncy exercise balls. It was bright yellow, reminding him of the sun. He wondered what she had in mind for it. He started to ask, but decided he would just use his imagination. The only problem was that the thoughts going through his mind were probably way off from what she'd intended.

He looked back over at her and saw she was pretty absorbed in what she was doing. He glanced back down at the ball, then back at her again. *Imagine.* He could see her naked, with her back on the ball. She'd be spread across it, facing him. Thighs open, her femininity wet and ready as he straddled her. And when she arched her body upward, he would lower his downward to connect. It would be a joining he would savor as he fought not to push too hard nor too fast inside of her. Sensations would take over and pleasure would seep into their pores, sink hard into their bones and—

"If the reason you're standing there staring at the ball is because you're trying to figure out where it goes, don't bother. It's not supposed to be in here. I use it to exercise."

He glanced over at her. "I was just imagining you working out on it." He shifted his gaze back to the ball and then returned it to her with a lazy smile. "So, what do you say, Alpha? Do you want to play ball?"

Fourteen

Two days later, Alpha tried to downplay both her nerves and her excitement as Riley escorted her into McKay's to meet his family. Although she kept reminding herself that her purpose for being here was mainly to bring everyone up to date on the holiday party, she could barely contain her enthusiasm.

Riley had ended up spending Monday night with her and had dropped by for dinner last night, as well. She'd had that couple's seventieth anniversary party for Valentine's Day to work on, and while she sat at the kitchen table taking care of the details for that event, he had stretched out on her living room floor in front of the fireplace, watching a cop show on television.

He had pretty much left her alone to hammer out the details for the February party, but, from where she sat at the kitchen table, she could see him. She had been fully aware of each time he'd moved, whether it was to stand to stretch his legs or to shift his body into another position on the floor.

When she had finally finished her work, she had joined

him in front of the fireplace with glasses of wine. Later they'd stripped each other naked and made love before he left at midnight.

She was well aware that time was ticking. They had less than three weeks before their affair would end. Since the finale was the night of the party, she was reminded of it each time she worked on the holiday celebration.

"Well, hello, Riley. Welcome to McKay's," a feminine voice said. Alpha glanced up at their hostess and saw it was the same woman from before.

"Paula," Riley greeted. "I believe my family is here already."

"Yes, they are," the woman said, in a cheerful mood, deliberately not looking at Alpha. "Must be an important business meeting going on with your family."

"No, just our usual get-together," Riley said, handing Paula his leather jacket and then proceeding to help Alpha out of her coat to hand over to Paula, as well.

Alpha wondered why the woman blinked and stared at her so hard, roaming her gaze up and down Alpha's outfit. The ankle-length, formfitting dress Alpha was wearing had been one she'd purchased while shopping in Memphis. She could tell from the way Riley had looked her up and down when he'd picked her up, and the low whistle that had eased from his lips, that he liked the way she looked. So what was this woman's problem? Why was this Paula checking Alpha out with venom in her eyes? It wasn't hard to figure out there was history between Paula and Riley. Alpha had picked up on that the last time.

But then a part of her understood any woman giving Riley a second glance on any night. But especially tonight. The man looked so jaw-droppingly, potently sexy, so robustly masculine, in his Armani jeans, herringbone blazer and white shirt.

She was tempted to tell Paula to pull back her fangs. In a few more weeks, Riley would be on the eligibility list once again. That meant this woman might be the next woman in his bed.

As Alpha studied the woman's reaction further, she saw Paula turn her stunned expression to Riley, who merely smiled. Alpha couldn't help wondering if there was a private joke somewhere, and if there was, why it seemed to involve her.

She glanced over at Riley, who broke eye contact with the woman to glance over at her. A different smile touched his lips when he slid his hand in hers and asked, "Ready?"

She drew in a deep breath and tried dismissing from her mind the interaction she'd seen pass between Riley and Paula. She returned his smile. "Yes, I'm ready."

He then looked back at Paula. "Please show us to our table."

Alpha saw the stiffening of the woman's spine as she moved forward to do as Riley had asked. Paula might be ticked off, but that didn't stop her from deliberately swaying her hips in her short black waitress outfit as she led them toward the back of the restaurant. Alpha was sure Paula's saucy walk was for Riley's benefit.

When they reached the room, Paula opened the door and stepped aside. The look she slanted Alpha would have cut her to the core had she thought the situation was that serious. To her, it wasn't. Alpha thought it was simply pathetic for any woman to get pissed off at another woman over a man neither of them had any right to claim.

They stepped into the room and all the conversation between the people at the long table suddenly ceased as all eyes shifted toward her and Riley. The men stood and the women eyed her and Riley curiously. She knew Megan was expecting her, but she hoped her presence wasn't a surprise to everyone else. Surely Riley had told his family he had invited her. Therefore, Alpha could only assume the reason they were staring with such intensity was because Riley was still holding her hand and didn't seem inclined to release it.

Seizing the moment when they had everyone's attention, Riley said, "Hello, everyone. I'd like for you to meet Alpha Blake."

Alpha waited for him to continue the introduction, expecting him to say something like "Alpha is the event planner handling our company's holiday party." But he provided no further clarification as he tightened his hand on hers and moved around the table, making individual introductions. Because he had talked about his family so much, she felt like she knew them already.

Everybody shifted places and she found herself sitting with Riley on one side of her and his brother, Canyon, on the other. To say the Westmoreland men favored was an understatement. Because she knew Dillon and Pam already, she felt comfortable being included in the conversations. Other than being asked where she was from—which led to a discussion about Florida beaches—no one inquired about anything concerning her family and she was grateful for that.

Riley helped tremendously by being so attentive. At some points, she wondered if he was overdoing it, since more than one of his brothers and cousins took note of it. When he asked her to try what he'd ordered for dinner, he had fed it to her with his fork and then used that same fork to finish eating his meal.

"Are you excited about planning the party, Alpha?" Riley's cousin Bailey asked from across the table.

Alpha smiled and nodded. "Yes, definitely, and I think all of you will be pleased." Bailey had been making conversation with Alpha off and on during the meal and it was hard to believe the young woman was the same one Riley had claimed was once a holy terror in the Westmoreland family.

It was later that evening, when Riley was taking her back home after dinner, that she decided to bring up that very thing with him. Although he didn't take his eyes off the road, she saw the way his lips curved in a smile.

"Don't let the sweet act fool you. I would be the first to admit that Bailey has matured in a lot of ways, but if rubbed the wrong way, the old Bailey will resurface in a minute. I'm surprised she took to you so easily. Usually she's very stand offish with those who aren't family."

"Then I guess I should feel special."

The car came to a stop at a traffic light and he turned his dark, piercing gaze toward her. The moment their eyes connected, she almost forgot to breathe. The kind of heat she was beginning to get accustomed to around him curled around in her stomach, making her nipples stiffen and her pulse rate increase.

"You are special, Alpha."

She had to draw in a deep breath, wondering why on earth he had to go and say something like that. Why had he spoken in that husky voice that could make her panties wet on impact? And why did she want to believe he actually thought she was someone special?

"Thank you," was the only response she could make. Her heart was beating a mile a minute. Riley had the ability to make her want things she shouldn't. Believe in things that she couldn't. Hadn't she learned her lesson with LeBron and Eddie? But still, she wished she could ask Riley to explain what he meant. Why he thought she was special. Heaven help her, she really didn't want to put too much stock into what he'd just said.

Riley turned his attention back to the road and she let out a deep sigh. No matter how many times he looked at her or touched her, her body responded in a way it had never responded to a man before. Her affair with him was supposed to be just a fling that meant nothing. Sex with no commitment

She swallowed with difficulty. But she was beginning to

feel emotions that she shouldn't be feeling, especially when she knew the score.

That wasn't good.

Riley settled between Alpha's thighs and gazed down at her as he lifted her hips to ease unerringly into the essence of her. They stared at each other, looking deeply into each other's eyes, as he guided his throbbing erection right through her heat.

He released a low growl the moment her muscles began clenching him, pulling him deeper inside of her, sending frissons of pleasure rippling all through him. What was there about how she made him feel, the emotions making love to her evoked?

Riley closed his eyes as he began moving, slowly thrusting in and out of her. He didn't want to rush. He wanted to savor the moment. His body felt alive, free. Tension began flowing out of him, unwinding and easing away to allow sexual gratification to come in to such a degree that he flexed his toes in time with his strokes. This was what real lovemaking was about, the kind that made you realize what you'd been missing, and what you could only have when you loved a woman.

What the... He snatched his eyes open to look down at her and was grateful to find her eyes closed as a deep moan escaped from between her lips. Something made her open her eyes and her sultry gaze connected to his. He knew there was no way he could deny what he was feeling at that moment. Emotions he didn't want to feel. And he was certain they were the same kind of emotions that had torn Bane's heart in two.

But he was feeling them nonetheless.

There was no way he could deny that he had fallen in love with Alpha.

He had felt himself falling hard in Memphis, probably even before that. And each time he'd tried fighting it and denying it, he was drawn to her even more. He knew his family had

questions since he'd never invited any woman to their little
family gatherings before. By arriving with her tonight, he
had made a statement. He was taking a chance with his heart.

A part of him wanted to believe Alpha was different. She
would never hurt him the way Crystal had hurt Bane. But
what about those family secrets she was obviously trying
to keep? He brushed the thought aside. Whatever they were
didn't matter. He loved her anyway.

His body kept moving inside of her, boldly claiming what
he deemed, at that moment, would always belong to him.
Starting tonight, he would be a Westmoreland in pursuit. He
knew there were things she wasn't ready to share with him
and that was fine; he would use his time to break down her
defenses and prove to her that no matter what had happened
in the past, he was a man worthy of her love.

Overcome with emotions he couldn't contain, he tightened
his hold on her and leaned down to capture her mouth with
his. It was either that or confess words she was not ready to
hear.

She locked her legs tighter around him and he heard her
deep groan at the same time as sensations burst within him,
releasing spasms of pleasure that ripped all through him. Shot
to every angle of his body.

He broke off the kiss to throw his head back. "Alpha!"

And then he exploded, spurting his release all through
her as he encountered an out-of-body experience that connected him to her in a way that tested the bedsprings. He felt
vibrant, alert, alive, and now he also knew how it felt to be
a man in love.

As his tremors subsided, he eased off Alpha, lifted her
in his arms and snuggled her head to his chest. Their bodies
were wet with sweat and their limbs entwined as he gathered
her closer. They were connected heart to heart, soul to soul.
He knew that no matter how long it took to convince her, Alpha's place in his life was permanent.

Fifteen

"Are you excited about the party this weekend?"

Alpha glanced up from her inventory list and smiled over at Lindsey. Her question was bittersweet. Yes, Alpha usually loved the day an event she'd worked on finally arrived, but since this event also meant the end of her affair with Riley, she was torn.

She decided to give Lindsey the answer her assistant probably expected to hear. "Yes, I'm excited."

She immediately glanced back down at her list so Lindsey wouldn't see the tears threatening to fall whenever she thought about what this weekend entailed. It was hard to believe it had been three weeks since her trip with Riley to Memphis. So much had happened since then. First, it had been his invitation to McKay's to meet his family. She was certain that is what had prompted Pam to call her two days later to invite her to the Westmorelands' Thanksgiving dinner.

Every one of the Denver Westmorelands had been there except for Bane and his cousin Gemma who lived in Australia. The twins, Aiden and Adrian, had schooled her on the family's after-Thanksgiving-dinner game of snow volleyball. Lucky for everyone, except for her, it had snowed that morning and a sufficient amount was still on the ground after dinner. After the players divided into the Reds and the Blues, she found her and Riley on opposite teams.

It had been the most fun she'd had in a long time, and she'd seen just how down-to-earth the Westmorelands were. For a little while, they had made her feel like she was a part of them. That was one of the reasons breaking up with Riley was going to be so hard.

Then there was also the fact that she had fallen in love with him.

As she continued to check items off her list, she couldn't help but feel the pain in her heart. Omega had warned her that such a thing could happen as soon as the flowers began arriving. The day after she'd had dinner with his family at McKay's, he had, for no reason at all, begun sending her flowers. The flowers would arrive practically every two to three days and when she asked why, he would merely smile and say it was because he was thinking about her.

Then there were those other habits they had started that would be hard to break—like sharing dinner practically every day, either at her place or his; his spending the nights with her more often than not; and their Friday date-nights. They would take in a movie or go to a play or roller-skating. More than once, he had mentioned something about her going skiing with him and she would change the subject, not having the heart to remind him that they wouldn't be together for the trip to Aspen that he had planned for January.

An hour or so later, after Lindsey had left, Alpha was busy making last-minute adjustments to the menu for this weekend's party when her phone rang. She smiled when she saw it was Riley.

"Hi. Thanks for the flowers. You are spoiling me."

"You deserve to be spoiled. I just want to make sure we're still on for tonight."

"Most certainly. I always enjoy any meals you cook." They would be dining at his place and, as usual, she would be spending the night.

"I have a special dish for you."

She chuckled. "What is it?"

"A surprise."

She liked his surprises. "All right."

"Good. I left work at noon today to come home to get things together, so I'll come and get you—"

"There's no need for you to do that, Riley. I can drive over to your place...unless you have a problem with my car being seen by anyone."

"Why would I have a problem with it?"

"I'm staying the night, remember. I wouldn't want your family to—"

"What I do is my business. Trust me, they know we're involved and have probably seen your car here overnight before. Do you have a problem with them knowing?"

"No, I don't have a problem with it, not at all," she said.

"Good. In that case, I'll see you when you get here."

She hung up the phone, thinking that even if she had a problem with it, it was too late. Time wasn't on her side and she wanted to spend as much of it with Riley as possible.

Riley had just finished everything and had put the stew on to simmer when he heard the sound of his doorbell. He glanced at his watch. He wasn't expecting Alpha for another hour or so and hoped it wasn't one of his relatives dropping in without calling first. Some of them could smell his stew from miles away and thought it was their God-given right to invite themselves over for a free meal.

As he walked out of the kitchen toward his front door, he couldn't help but smile. He was looking forward to Alpha coming over because, at some time before she left in the morning, he wanted to tell her just how he felt. The holiday party was in three days, and he needed to hear from her that although she might not have fallen in love with him yet, the idea was possible.

Without checking to see who his caller was, he snatched open his door. A deep frown settled on his face when he saw Paula standing on his porch. "Paula, what are you doing here?"

She smiled brightly. "I came to see you, of course. I have some information that I think you need to know."

Riley doubted it and was about to tell her so when she quickly slid by him to enter his house. Closing the door behind him, he crossed his arms over his chest and watched her look around like she'd never been here before, and then he remembered she hadn't. He had broken things off with her before the affair had gotten that far. "What information do I need to know?"

She turned to face him and threw her hair back from her face. She was wearing knee-high leather boots and a light blue mini sweater dress that was so tight it appeared glued to her body. "Mmm, something smells good. Don't you want to invite me to dinner?" she asked, placing her hands on her hips to draw attention to her small waistline.

At that moment, he admired Alpha even more. During the time they'd spent together, she'd never found any reason to flaunt her attributes. They were noticeable without her having to show them off. "Sorry, I'm expecting company in a few hours."

He saw the frown settle on her face. "I take it that you're still involved with that party planner," she said with a sneer.

He tried keeping his anger in check. "What of it?"

"You must like her a lot to include her in one of your family dinners. Not too many women get that privilege from Riley Westmoreland. I didn't. And I know how much you pride yourself on your reputation and the family's name and all that."

He wondered what she was getting at. "If you have something to say, Paula, just say it."

"All right, then." She paused a moment and then slid down to sit on his sofa uninvited, crossing her legs, deliberately showing plenty of thigh and said, "I'm sure you've heard I'm seeing Samuel Porter."

Not that he cared, but he wasn't surprised. Sam was and always had been a party animal, and Paula liked having a good time and getting wild and crazy. And he'd heard Sam was into over-the-top stuff in the bedroom, like group sex and all that. "And?"

"And I was going through Sam's collection of special videos one night to pick out one I thought we would enjoy watching together. Get my drift?"

Riley did get her drift and didn't have to ask what Sam's special videos were. He'd heard the rumor years ago that Sam had a cabinet filled with porn. He drew in a deep breath, still not sure where she was going with all of this. "And?"

"And…" she said, smiling, pulling something out of her purse, "I came across one, and the woman looked so familiar that I took a second look. You might want to take a look, as well. I'm sure you'll recognize her."

He took the DVD she offered and glanced at the picture of the couple, mainly the woman who was stretched out spread-eagle on a four-poster bed very naked. His heart nearly stopped beating, and he forced his hand to stop trembling. He looked at Paula, fighting to keep his teeth from gnashing together in anger. "What are you trying to insinuate?"

"That your girlfriend used to have a naughty past."

He tossed the DVD on the sofa next to her. "I think you're about to set yourself up for a lawsuit you can't afford. This is not my girlfriend on this DVD jacket, just someone who favors her."

Paula lifted her chin dubiously and smiled. "You sure of that?"

Riley's gaze narrowed. Yes, he was sure. The porn star on the DVD jacket was not Alpha.

"Positive. In fact I'm so positive that if I hear about this from anyone else, I'm going to assume you're the one spreading vicious lies and malicious gossip, and I will sue you myself for slandering her name."

The smile quickly disappeared from her face. "You wouldn't do that."

"Try me."

She drew in a deep breath. "I know what I see."

"And I know what I know, but if you want to play your hand, go ahead, I dare you. I won't stop until I make you not only a laughingstock but destitute. Now, I want you to leave and not come back. And remember what I said. If I get wind of any lies you're spreading, I will make sure you regret it."

She jerked up off the sofa and angrily headed for the door, opened it and slammed it shut behind her with enough force to make his windows shake. It was only then that he noticed she'd left the DVD behind, whether accidentally or intentionally he wasn't sure.

Picking up the DVD he headed for the bedroom to take a shower. His dinner guest would be arriving within the hour. And he knew just as sure as the forecasters had predicted snow for the weekend that at some point during the course of the evening, he and Alpha would have a long talk.

"We need to talk, Alpha."

Alpha glanced over at Riley. Something was wrong; she could feel it. Although dinner had been great and she enjoyed his company as usual, she was chilled by the feeling that something just wasn't right. More than once during dinner she had caught Riley staring at her only to quickly look away. What was going on?

A part of her didn't want to know, but still she couldn't stop the what-ifs from swimming through her head. What if he wanted to bring a date Saturday night and had decided he wanted to end his affair a few days early? He had been so adamant about her having dinner with him this evening and now she couldn't help wondering if it was one of those break-up meals. Men had a way of thinking a woman preferred to get dumped on a full stomach. Hadn't Eddie taken her to dinner the night before he'd given her the ultimatum about Omega?

"Alpha."

She took a sip of her wine before placing her glass down on the table. She was a big girl and could handle anything that came her way. But she didn't want to do it now. If he wanted to make this their last night together then she wanted it to be special.

Easing up off the sofa, she slowly crossed the room to where he sat in a leather wingback chair. With his legs stretched out in front of him, he was sipping his own wine while his dark, penetrating gaze watched her every move. And with good reason, she thought, since she was discarding her clothes, piece by piece. His attention was definitely being held the way she wanted it to be. They would have their talk but it would be later. Much later.

By the time she had reached his chair she was totally naked. He pulled her down in his lap and cradled her in his arms. "You like tempting me, don't you?" he asked huskily, leaning close to her lips.

"Umm, it wouldn't be any fun if I didn't." And she wanted him to remember all the times she had tempted him and he had tempted her. She wanted him to remember everything, especially when they were no longer involved. Because she would. Her memories would sustain her when she buried herself in her work to forget him.

It would be hard being involved with Megan's wedding.

She expected to run into him, but hopefully, she would have gotten over him by then.

Yet how could a woman get over a man she truly loved?

"Baby, we need to talk."

She leaned in close to him, and swiped the tip of her tongue across his lips. "And we will talk, Riley. Later. Now I want you to take off your clothes so we can have fun," she said, easing off his lap and pulling him up from the chair.

"Fun?" he asked her, reaching out and running his fingers across the tips of her breasts while letting his gaze roam all over her body.

"Yes," she said, looking up at him as she pulled his belt through the loops of his jeans and then began unbuttoning his shirt. "What do you say about that?"

He reached out and swept her off her feet and headed toward the stairs to his bedroom. "Then I'd say, let's get started."

Alpha stretched out her legs in bed the moment she opened her eyes. It was daylight, and through the window she saw it was lightly snowing. Just her luck, what with those last-minute details she had to handle to get ready for the party tomorrow night.

She turned over in the empty bed, wondering where Riley was. It was then that she saw the note pinned to the pillow where his head had lain the night before.

Didn't want to wake you, but I had an eight o'clock meeting at work. I know you probably have a ton of things to do today to get ready for tomorrow, but make yourself at home until you're ready to leave. Riley.

She held the note to her chest, thinking that at least he hadn't mentioned anything else about them talking. She flopped back down in bed as a smile touched her lips. She'd deliberately made him forget. All it took was for her to glance around at the rumpled bedcovers to know just where Riley Westmoreland's concentration had been last night and during the early hours of this morning. She hadn't gotten much sleep last night, which wouldn't be bad if she didn't have a million things to do.

She looked around the room for her clothes and then remembered she had removed them last night in the living room. The last thing she intended to do was parade around Riley's house naked. He mentioned that he never locked his doors and his brothers or cousins were known to just drop in. Easing out of the bed, she knew he had a robe around here someplace. When she didn't see one, she figured one of his T-shirts would have to do.

She recalled just where he kept them and opened the top drawer to his dresser. Her breath caught. Lying on top of his stack of T-shirts was a DVD, but not just any DVD. It was one of her sister's, titled *Time to Play*. Where did he get it? How long had he had it?

Alpha stood there staring at the DVD as a thousand questions flowed through her mind. Did Riley assume like LeBron had at first that it was her on the DVD and not Omega? Or did he figure like LeBron had later that if he couldn't have his ideal porn star then her twin sister would do?

She angrily shoved the drawer closed as fury ripped through her. No wonder he had wanted an affair with her.

But then why was she getting angry anyway? She'd known it was nothing but sex with no commitment all along. Nothing more.

Not caring anymore if anyone saw her naked, she raced downstairs and saw Riley had picked up her clothes off the floor and placed them on the sofa. She quickly dressed, grabbed her purse from the table and left. For the first time since moving to Denver, she didn't notice the cold.

What she noticed more than anything was how deep her heart was hurting.

Sixteen

Riley walked into the ballroom of the Pavilion Hotel and stopped short. Wow! Alpha had miraculously transformed the room into one winter's night, just as the theme declared.

The color scheme was silver, blue and white. Large white columns had been erected, connected by swathes of white netting. The ceiling looked like a midnight sky with the moon and dots of stars. Miniature mounds of snow lay in one area and props of snow-covered mountains were strategically placed around the room.

"Welcome." A hostess dressed as a snow maiden greeted him. "And here's your gift from Blue Ridge Management," she said, handing him a snow globe with a replica of the Blue Ridge Management building inside.

"Thanks." He couldn't resist shaking it up and watching snow float all around. A huge smile touched his lips. His woman had definitely outdone herself. *Imagine.*

"Your girlfriend did a bang-up job, didn't she?"

He turned and looked into Bailey's smiling face. He could tell she was equally impressed. "Yes, she did."

Bailey tilted her head. "So, she is your girlfriend?"

He paused, thinking that Bailey was the second person in two days who had referred to Alpha as his girlfriend. He hadn't denied it then, and he wouldn't deny it now. "Yes, she's my girlfriend."

She stared at him. "Of all the women you've been involved with, I've never known you to claim any of them as anything other than a sleeping partner."

He grabbed a glass of wine from the tray of a passing waiter. Everything, including the outfits the waiters and waitresses wore, looked festive and right in keeping with the party's theme. "She's different."

"In that case, I hope you intend to treat her differently."

He already was, and would continue to do so. In fact, starting tonight, he intended for them to take their relationship to a whole new level, but first they needed to talk. He had left several messages, but she hadn't found time to return them. He knew how hard she had worked and planned for the party tonight, often staying up late and getting up early. But tonight she had to be proud of her accomplishments. He was, and was certain the rest of his family would be, as well.

"You look good, by the way," Bailey said, giving him a once-over. "You Westmoreland men clean up well."

He couldn't help but laugh. "So do Westmoreland women." He glanced around again. "Have you seen Alpha?"

"Yes. She's around here someplace, making sure everything is running smoothly. At some point, I hope you make sure she slows down to enjoy herself. She's worked hard for tonight and it shows."

It was a half hour later before he got a chance to see Alpha, and it was from across the room. He had been standing in a group talking to Morris Caper, one of the oldest employees at Blue Ridge, along with the man's wife, Canyon, Stern and two other couples, when Alpha came into his line of sight. His breath caught when he saw her. She was wearing blue, the same shade being used at the party.

He nodded a few times, trying to pretend to listen to the speaker, when in reality his attention was on Alpha. He began wondering why she wouldn't look his way. Surely she knew he'd arrived. However, he had to remind himself that tonight wasn't about him. She had a job to do. But he had a niggling discomfort that something wasn't right.

He was about to look back at Mr. Caper when Alpha finally glanced his way. He was about to give her a smile and a thumbs-up when the look she gave him made him go still. What was that glare all about? He lifted his brow, and she quickly turned to head toward the room where food was being prepared.

"Excuse me for a minute," he said to the group before walking off in the direction Alpha had gone. Something was going on, and he intended to find out what.

He walked through several rooms and was stopped by a number of people before he finally came within a few feet of her. She looked up, saw him and was about to walk away when he increased his pace and touched her arm. "Everything is above my expectations, Alpha, but I'd like to talk to you for a second."

He was very much aware that with others around, she couldn't deny his request. After all, his family was the one paying for this affair.

"All right."

To anyone else it would appear she was acknowledging his request, because, unless you were standing as close to her as he was, you couldn't see the sharp daggers in her eyes or the tightness of her lips. *What the hell?*

"Privately, please," he said, taking her arm and leading her to an empty room in the back, far away from her staff, his employees or his family members.

He closed the door behind them and then turned to her. She was looking at everything in the storage room but him. And he could feel her tension. Her anger. "Now. Would you like to tell me what's going on?"

Her brows furrowed, and she lifted her chin. "There's nothing going on, at least nothing you should be concerned about. This is our breakup night anyway, right? What did you say when we started out, that you didn't stay with any woman past six weeks? Well, your six weeks ended today, no sweat."

Riley gritted his teeth. "What's this about, Alpha?"

"Nothing, and if you don't mind, I have a party to run and—"

"Your assistant can handle things until you get back. And I intend to keep you here until you tell me what's wrong, even if it takes all night."

She placed her hands on her hips. "I don't owe you any explanations."

He crossed the room to where she stood in a furious stance with her gaze flaring, spine straight and head thrown back. "Yes, you do. When I left you in bed yesterday morning it was with a smile on your face, so what's with the venom tonight? Are you mad because I left without waking you?"

"Is that what you think?"

He rubbed his hand down his face. "I don't know what to think, so tell me."

Alpha tried not to give in to the plea she heard in his voice and turned her back to him. For two solid days she had tried putting thoughts of him out of her mind. She had tried to concentrate on what had to be done for this party. It hadn't been easy, but she had managed to get through it somehow, and every single Westmoreland here, including him, had complimented her on her work. Tonight should be a night of celebration and excitement for her. Instead it was one of heartbreak.

She heard him move and could feel his heat, breathe in his

masculine scent and knew he was standing directly behind her with little space between them. The thought of what he'd done and what he'd thought of her hit low and hard, and he had the nerve to act like nothing happened. In essence he had no idea what she'd found in his drawer. Maybe it was time for her to tell him.

She turned around and met his inquisitive gaze. "Yesterday morning after you left, I needed a T-shirt to put on before going downstairs to get my clothes."

"Go on."

"I thought you wouldn't mind if I looked in your drawer to get one."

Something in his gaze let her know that he knew what would come next and he spoke before she did. "And you found that DVD Paula gave me."

His words nearly sucked the breath from her lungs. "Paula?"

"Yes, Paula, from McKay's."

Her head began spinning. Now she understood the looks that had passed between him and Paula that night. "So that was the private joke between the two of you," she said, barely getting the words out, forcing them beyond the tears she refused to let fall.

"What are you talking about?"

"Nothing. The main thing right now is that you had that video and you thought it was me, didn't you? That's why you initiated an affair with me, isn't it? I played right into your hands—and into your bed."

Riley felt a sting to his cheek, thinking her words were like a slap to his face. He struggled against the need to lash out at her the way she was lashing out at him. How could she assume something like that? "What are you accusing me of, Alpha?"

"That you and your ex-girlfriend thought you had things

figured out. You both thought that I'm the woman on that porn DVD."

At that moment he felt angrier than he'd ever felt in his life because the woman he loved didn't trust him. She had a lot of nerve. He had been up-front with her about everything. She was the one keeping secrets yet he had fallen in love with her anyway, against his better judgment.

Risking the kind of pain he'd vowed never to feel.

"I knew you were not the woman on that jacket," he said through gritted teeth.

She took a step closer to him, got in his face. "How could you have known that when Omega is my identical twin? You wouldn't be the first man who thought I was her."

"I don't give a royal damn what other men thought. I knew it wasn't you the minute I looked at that DVD jacket. You might be identical twins but a man who has made love to you as often as I have, who has touched you, tasted you, got up close and personal with you, could tell the difference. I know every mole, crevice, indention and mark on your body. I knew that wasn't you and figured it had to be your twin…a twin you never told me you had."

He paused a moment and added, "And if you recall, I did mention we needed to talk and intended to bring it up on Thursday night, the same day Paula brought that DVD over for me to see. I told her then it wasn't you. So who's the victim here, Alpha? It seems pretty clear to me that I trusted you a whole hell of a lot more than you trusted me."

He then turned and walked out of the room.

Alpha drew in a deep breath the moment she heard the door close behind Riley. Was it really true? Had he known the woman on that DVD jacket wasn't her? If so, then she had done him a grave injustice, especially when she hadn't told him about Omega.

What had been lacking between them was trust and communication, more on her part than on his. He had told her about his family, introduced her to them, but she had told him hardly anything about hers. And he hadn't been quick to believe the worst about her like she had about him.

And he *had* wanted to talk Thursday night, but she'd assumed he wanted to break things off with her. Had she let him have his say, none of this would have happened, and if she hadn't jumped to conclusions and assumed the worst then she wouldn't be standing here filled with so much remorse. But after dealing with the likes of LeBron and Eddie, she had been too afraid to trust another man.

There was a gentle knock on the door. "Yes?"

Lindsey stuck her head in with a concerned look on her face. "Is everything all right?"

"Yes, why do you ask?"

She came into the room and shrugged. "I saw Mr. Westmoreland request to talk privately and wondered what could be wrong since everything seems to be going all right. Everyone I talked to thinks you outdid yourself. Everything is beautiful."

Alpha swallowed deeply. "I had a lot of help, and no, Mr. Westmoreland wasn't complaining about anything. He wanted to discuss another matter."

"Oh."

Deciding the best thing she could do now was to get back to work and stay busy, she said, "Come on. Let's make sure everything continues to stay impressive for everyone." She checked her watch. "It's almost time for the snow to start falling."

As part of the theme, she had decided to have fake snowflakes swirl from the ceiling, and with the special lightning she had installed, it would give the illusion that the entire ballroom had been transformed into a beautiful winter wonderland.

As Alpha left the room with Lindsey, she knew what she should do but had no idea how to go about it.

* * *

"You sure you don't want to come to dinner, Riley? With that huge snowstorm headed this way it might be the last good home-cooked meal you get for a while," Dillon said.

"Yes, it might be at that," Riley replied as he stood at the window and looked out. It hadn't started snowing yet but according to the forecasters a snowstorm was headed their way. "But I'll still pass. I wouldn't be much company anyway."

Dillon didn't say anything for a minute. "So Pam and Chloe were right. There's trouble in paradise."

Riley didn't have to figure out how they knew. He had found out a long time ago that the women in his family were too observant for their own good. "I guess you can say that."

"Then take it from someone who knows, people in love have spats sometimes."

Riley lifted his brow and said in a defensive tone, "Who said I was in love?"

"I did. And don't try denying it. I watched you and Alpha at the party trying to avoid each other. It's been over a week. Don't you think the two of you need to kiss and make up?"

Riley rolled his eyes. "Too complicated to kiss and make up, Dil."

"Not if you really love her. If I can forgive Pam for coming within seconds of marrying another man, then I'm certain you can forgive Alpha for whatever the transgression."

A short while later, after his conversation with his oldest brother had ended, Riley stood in the kitchen pouring a cup of coffee, replaying in his mind what Dillon had said. He appreciated the pep talk but there were times when it was better just to count your losses, move on and not look back. Instead, he was going to take the same advice he'd given to Bane—advice Bane had refused to follow. Now, his brother was *still* hurting and, more than ever, Riley refused to be another Bane.

He was about to walk over to the refrigerator to pull out a microwave dinner when he heard his doorbell. He didn't have to wonder who was probably at his door. Bailey. She'd called twice already and if Dillon had mentioned Riley planned on skipping a meal with the family, she wouldn't hesitate to come and grill him about things he'd rather not talk about.

He thought about not answering but decided if Bailey had braved the blistering cold to come to his place then he would see what she wanted. But he would not let her stay long. Although the snowstorm hadn't hit yet, it was cold as the dickens outside. He would send Bailey on her way, and he would eat his meal alone and get in bed early. The mayor had already predicted that most of Denver, including the airport, would be shut down tomorrow.

Riley opened the door to find this furry white thing standing in front of him. He leaned in the doorway, trying to make out just what or who it was when the person tilted her head and moved away all the fur. "Alpha?"

She nodded. "May I come in so we can talk? It's cold out here."

He quickly moved aside. "Get near the fireplace," he ordered, wondering what in the world she was doing out in this weather. It was in the low teens. He thought it was pretty damn cold and he was used to it. It would be murder on someone like her.

He stood back and watched as she peeled off a long white coat trimmed in fur with a matching hat and gloves. She then pulled a white knitted ski mask from her face before pulling off another coat and two sweaters. When she stood trembling in front of the fireplace in a pair of winter-white stretched slacks and a pretty winter-white pullover turtleneck sweater, he just stared. The outfit looked good on her. Too good.

And when she ran her fingers through her hair to fluff it out, he felt heat on his skin. He swallowed hard and said, "I'll pour you a cup of coffee while you warm up. And then you can tell me why you came here in all this bad weather."

He quickly walked away, to the kitchen, and tried to

breathe calmly while he poured her coffee. He hadn't seen her or talked to her since the party, but that didn't mean he hadn't thought about her, because he had—every waking minute as well as when he should have been sleeping. She hated cold weather, yet she had come here, on what would probably be the coldest day they'd had since last winter.

Trying to keep his hand steady, he walked back to the living room and found her standing with her back to him, in front of the fireplace, staring down at the flames as if she was in deep thought. He wondered what she was thinking about and knew he would soon find out.

"Here you are," he said, claiming her attention. She crossed the room to meet him. She took the cup from his hand and the minute their fingers touched, a frisson of warmth flowed through him. He took a step back and watched as she immediately took a sip.

She glanced up at him. "Thanks, I needed that."

"I'm sure you did. So why are you here, Alpha?"

"I was hoping we could talk. I considered calling but figured you would refuse."

She had figured right. "What more is there to say? I trusted you more than you trusted me."

"It's not just about trust, Riley."

He crossed his arms over his chest. "Then what else is there?"

"An understanding between us. And I would be the first to admit I didn't tell you everything, but I had a reason for keeping my family secrets to myself. All we were sharing was an affair."

She glanced over at the sofa. "May I sit down so we can talk? I think it's time that I tell you everything."

A part of him was tempted to tell her no. It was too late to tell him everything. He preferred that she leave.

But he knew he couldn't say any of that. She had come over in the cold weather, which meant whatever she had to say was important to her. So the least he could do was listen to what she had to say. "Yes, you may have a seat."

She sat down and he took the chair across from her and wondered why she hadn't been able to decipher when his feelings for her had changed and he'd wanted more than sex without a commitment. What had she thought those flowers were all about, the amount of time he had spent with her compared to all the others?

He watched her and knew she was trying to gather her thoughts. Why? Was he such a hard guy to talk to? He had shared more of himself with her than with any other woman. Too bad he couldn't say the same about her.

She looked over at him, met his gaze and he knew he had lied to himself.

He'd awakened that morning with a firm resolve that he no longer wanted her or loved her. But seeing her here at Riley's Station only confirmed that he still wanted her in a way he'd never wanted another woman. And, more than anything, he still loved her.

She finally began talking. "My identical twin sister, Omega, dropped out of college our first year when she met this older guy at some club near campus. The man convinced her she should be a model."

She paused a moment and took another sip of her coffee. "Omega was always the more outgoing of the two of us and always wanted that sort of thing—the limelight, recognition, stardom—so her decision didn't surprise me. And, in a way, I doubt that it surprised my parents. At least it shouldn't have, since she was the one who defied their every order while we were growing up.

"Anyway, my parents were livid about her dropping out of college. When she left they didn't hear from her for months, but because she and I are close, I knew her whereabouts. I knew before anyone when she discovered the man hadn't propositioned her for a real modeling job but for a job as a porn star. He didn't twist her arm or hold her hostage. Omega could have walked away at any time. It was a choice she made. She thought she had a beautiful body, and she didn't mind flaunting it. She considered what she was doing a job. She was a well-paid entertainer and nothing else."

He nodded. "Did your parents know what she was doing?"

She shook her head. "No, and Omega and I both figured that they wouldn't find out, either. She was living out in California and had become popular on the West Coast; whereas my parents lived in Florida, the Bible Belt. We thought good churchgoing people would never find out about stuff like that. But we were wrong. It seemed a few men who knew my parents were getting porn off the internet, so you can just imagine how they couldn't wait to spread the word. Soon it got back to my parents. Someone even sent them a DVD in the mail."

"That was kind of low," he said.

"Yes, it was, and it led to a full-blown scandal that embarrassed my parents. Some of their so-called friends stopped socializing with them and, for a while, they lost business at the vet clinic. Mom and Dad tried to talk to Omega. Of course they went about it the wrong way, by making demands, and that only made her defiant. In the end, they threatened to cut her off if she didn't quit what she was doing and return home. They also forbade me to have contact with Omega, which I refused to do."

"I'm sure they weren't happy about that."

She shook her head. "No, they weren't. They finally just left me alone and requested that I not ever mention anything about Omega to them. The embarrassment was too much, and in the end they made a decision to disown her until she came to her senses."

She took another sip of her coffee. "A few years later, I met this guy name LeBron, who moved to Daytona with his job from Ohio," she said softly. "LeBron and I dated for six months, and I thought everything was going great until one night he presented me with one of my sister's DVDs and said he'd been a fan of hers for a couple of years. He even said what had drawn him to me was that he assumed I was her. And when he found out I wasn't, he figured he had the next best thing. He wanted me to imitate what she did on the DVD. He even wanted to call me Omega whenever we made love."

Riley tensed and anger flowed through his body. "He actually wanted you to pretend you were your sister?"

"Yes. I refused to do so and left. The next day he called, breaking things off with me."

She didn't say anything for a long minute. "A year later, I met Eddie when he brought his dog into the clinic. We hit it off immediately. He had moved to Daytona from his family's home in Palm Beach. They owned a slew of electronics shops, and he'd moved to Daytona to open a new store there. It was hard for me to trust anyone, and after we'd dated awhile, I told him everything. I confided about Omega and told him about LeBron. He was angry that LeBron could be such an ass, and he said what Omega did for a living meant nothing to him. It was her life and he could understand me wanting to keep a relationship with my sister."

"Sounds like a nice guy."

"I thought so, and when he asked me to marry him, I agreed. Everything was going along fine until someone, not sure who, sent his parents a copy of Omega's DVD. They were appalled and demanded that he end things with me. He refused, but they put pressure on him to at least get me to agree not to have anything to do with Omega."

She took another sip of coffee. "I refused, and he called off the wedding a week before it was to take place."

She paused, as if remembering that time. "That was another embarrassment for my parents, especially when they thought I should have given in to Eddie's request. I decided to move as far away as I could, which brought me to Denver."

He leaned forward. "So when you saw that DVD in my drawer, you assumed I was another LeBron or that I could be another Eddie?"

She held his gaze. "Yes."

Her single answer gave him pause. "Is that the reason you didn't talk much about your family?"

"Yes. I know all families have issues but to this day my parents have not forgiven my sister. If they had their way I wouldn't have any contact with her. My mother is softening somewhat. She at least asks about Omega. But my father is still being hard-nosed."

"Is your sister still in the business?"

"No, she quit making porn movies a few years ago, but some people have long memories, especially since she was once very popular. I've been on business trips when men have approached me asking if I was Omega and could they have my autograph."

She paused again. "I still don't understand it. You say you knew immediately it wasn't me, but that's hard to believe when most people can't tell me and Omega apart."

He nodded. "The first thing I noticed was the dye job."

She lifted a brow. "The dye job?"

"Yes, you once mentioned you'd never dyed your hair and it was obvious the woman on the DVD jacket had. And then when I looked at it further, I noticed she had a mole on her inner right thigh. You don't. And you don't have a tattoo near your navel."

She nodded. "I'm sorry about jumping to conclusions, Riley, but we had agreed on a sex-only relationship because the last thing I wanted was to get seriously involved with someone. I had before—twice— and things didn't work out."

"What is your sister doing now?"

"Omega is living in Paris and is happily married to a wonderful guy who knows about her past and loves her regardless. Marlon is a successful businessman and the two of them travel a lot. With his encouragement, she returned to school and now has her graduate degree. But even with her marriage and her other accomplishments and achievements, my parents still haven't forgiven her."

"And I take it your father wants you and Eddie to get back together."

Her eyes widened. "How do you know that?"

"If you recall, I happened to call you one day and you thought I was your father. You said something that let me know he was trying to get you to reinstate your relationship with your ex-fiancé."

"Yes, but only because Eddie thinks he still has a chance to convince me not to have anything to do with Omega. But like I told him, my sister and I are closer than ever."

"I'm glad."

She looked surprised. "You are?"

"Yes, and I'm disappointed you would think that I wouldn't be. I love family, Alpha. I told you about Bane, the twins and Bailey and the reputation they had around town. Not once did any one of us think about disowning them. You don't disown family, and I think it's sad that your parents are doing that to your sister. Nobody is perfect."

"Yes, but having a bad reputation around town for things you did while growing up is one thing, Riley. Being a porn star is another, and Eddie's family let me know that families with good names wouldn't want to have theirs tarnished by such a scandal. Why would I even assume your family would be any different?"

"Because you met them. We aren't judgmental nor do we place ourselves on any type of pedestal. There are skeletons in every family closet. I told you all the stuff we're uncovering on my grandfather Raphel."

He paused a moment and then asked, "Have you ever heard of the Chamberlain gang?"

She nodded. "Yes. Father and two sons did a rash of bank

robberies across the country some years back. I was in high school, and one of my classmates brought in an article about them. We all found it fascinating how they were able to pull things off, zigzagging across state lines and evading the FBI for as long as they did before finally getting caught."

"What they did was pretty scandalous, wouldn't you say?"

"Yes, of course."

"Well, I happen to know one of their family members. Brooke Chamberlain. The Chamberlain gang consisted of her father and her two older brothers. They're still serving time, and I doubt they will be getting out anytime soon."

"You actually know someone related to them?"

"Yes, in fact I know her very well because she's married to my cousin Ian Westmoreland, who owns a casino near Lake Tahoe. All of us know about Brooke's family but none of us hold it against her. We're also aware she keeps in contact with them and find no fault in that, as well. Family is family, Alpha. I would never have judged you by what your sister did. Nor would I have pushed you not to have any contact with her."

"I see that now, but because I wasn't sure, I didn't want to take the chance."

"Do you believe me?" he asked, holding her gaze steadily, with single-minded focus. He knew at that moment how much he wanted her to believe him. To believe in him.

"Yes. I didn't know then," she said softly. "But I do now."

He nodded, satisfied with her answer. "Now that we've cleared up your issues, let's discuss mine."

Dread rippled down Alpha's spine. She wondered just what kind of issues he could have. "All right."

He slowly stood from the chair and paced a few times in front of the fireplace. The glow from the fire reflected on him. In jeans and a pullover sweater, he looked too sexy for her senses. She watched him move and her stomach tightened with each step he took. Moments later, he stopped and turned to face her. "I told you about Bane and Crystal, right?"

She nodded. "Yes."

"What I didn't tell you was how much their fiery relationship affected me. Bane loved Crystal with the passion and soul of a man beyond his years. I felt the love whenever he mentioned her or when he would look at her. We all did, and that worried us. In a way, I felt sorry for Mr. Newsome. The more he tried keeping them apart, the more they were determined to stay together at any cost."

He was silent for a moment. "I saw the pain Bane went through when he and Crystal were forced apart. I can still see that pain whenever he comes home and asks about her or mentions her name. A love that fierce scared the hell out of me. I never wanted that kind of love for myself. Our lives were shattered when we lost our parents and uncle and aunt in that plane crash. I could not imagine falling in love with a woman and going through that sort of pain due to death or any other kind of separation."

He went back and sat down. "So my issues were making it hard for me to ever consider a serious involvement with a woman. Until you. With you, it was hard to keep my emotions in check, and I found myself wanting things I felt I shouldn't have."

Alpha could barely breathe. Was he saying what she hoped he was saying? That at some point it had become more than just sex with no commitment? That he had been fighting his emotions for her like she had been fighting hers for him? "What are you saying?" she asked softly.

"I'm saying that as much as I wished otherwise, it stopped being just sex for me during our trip to Memphis. I wanted to tell you then but didn't want to push you into anything. So I decided to give you hints about where I wanted our relationship to go. That's why I started sending the flowers. Why I invited you to meet my family. They took the hint but you

were slow. It angered me when Paula showed up at my plac
with that DVD. How could you have thought it had been
private joke between her and me?"

She tried to get her heart rate to slow down. Had he kin
of said, in so many words, that he loved her? "I saw the ex
change between you two that day at McKay's, when I too
off my coat and she saw my outfit."

He smiled. "Oh, that. It wasn't a private joke. It was eg
on her face. The last time she saw you, you were overdresse
because of the cold weather. She made a comment about m
dating a frumpy woman. She got to see just how *not* frump
you were and was almost rendered speechless. I liked the fac
that she had to eat crow."

"Oh."

"I think we both had misgivings about allowing our rela
tionship to go beyond anything other than just sex. So nov
I want to make it clear what I want. I want you, Alpha, an
not just in a physical way. I love you so damn much it scare
me. But I'm willing to take a chance on love and believe
was meant for us to be together, no matter what."

Alpha tried to fight back the tears that filled her eyes. "Ol
Riley, I love you, too, but I had promised myself never to le
anyone come between me and Omega. When I saw that DVI
in your drawer, I thought the worst and I'm sorry."

He eased from the chair and crossed the room to sit dow
beside her on the sofa. Reaching out, he wiped away her tear
and then took her hand in his and held it tight. "So what d
you think we should do about our issues?"

She was filled with so many emotions, she almost couldn'
speak. Then she said, "What do you suggest?"

"I think we need to communicate more when it come
to things that threaten the love we have for each other. Th
thought of losing you for any reason is my worst nightmar
and something I won't let happen."

"Oh, Riley."

He leaned down and brushed a kiss across her lips. Then he pulled her into his arms and kissed her with all the intense emotion that he was feeling. When he finally released her mouth, he softly caressed her cheek. "Will you marry me?"

She reached up and caressed his chin. "Only if we can have a long engagement. We owe it to ourselves to build our relationship, develop open communication and trust. And besides, there's no way we can marry before Megan's big day in June."

He nodded in agreement. "Then you decide when and I shall be there. I love you, and I want to spend the rest of my life with you."

"I love you, too." She stood. "Now I need to get back home before the storm hits."

He stood, as well. "If you think for one minute I'm letting you go back out in that weather, then think again. It's hard to believe you even ventured out."

"We needed to talk and I wanted to do it face-to-face."

"Well, we did, face-to-face, and you know what I think?"

"No."

"That our very own one winter's night should start now," he said, standing and pulling her close to him. "What do you say to that?"

She wrapped her arms around his neck. "I would say start the party."

He swept her off her feet and headed upstairs toward the bedroom, intending on doing just that.

Epilogue

A beautiful day in June

Riley grabbed Alpha's arm when she hurriedly walked by him and pulled her behind a huge planter to steal a quick kiss. "Hey, slow down. How long will I have to be without a date?"

Alpha wrapped her arms around Riley's neck. "Just long enough for Megan and Rico to cut the cake. Don't you think they made a beautiful bridal couple?"

"Yes, and thanks to Imagine, it was a storybook wedding. You truly outdid yourself. I thought everything was perfect."

"I think you're perfect." And she really meant that. Over the course of the past six months, she and Riley had continued to build an even stronger relationship. Somehow he had talked her into that ski trip to Aspen in January and, as promised, he had kept her warm…most of the time. She hadn't gotten the hang of being on skis but the evenings spent in his arms in front of the fireplace had given them plenty more winter nights to cherish.

He had flown home to Daytona Beach with her over Easter weekend to meet her parents. Before that, he had invited Omega and Marlon to a surprise party he'd given for Alpha at the end of February to celebrate her selection as Denver's Small Businesswoman of the Year. She could tell he liked Omega and was one of the few who could tell them apart. And Alpha knew Riley liked Marlon Farmer, Omega's husband. The two had hit it off immediately. Already plans were in the works for her and Riley to visit Omega and Marlon in Paris…especially since Omega was expecting. She had never seen her sister looking so happy and radiant.

She glanced down on the beautiful ring she wore. They had decided on an August wedding, and she was looking forward to becoming Mrs. Riley Westmoreland.

Alpha also knew that while in Daytona, Riley had talked with her parents and let them know that she had his full support in maintaining a close relationship with her twin. He further told them how much family meant to him and that he hoped one day they would be able to repair their relationship with Omega. She had fallen more in love with him at that moment.

The sound of loud laughter made Alpha look in the direction of the wedded couple. They had just cut the cake. After Megan fed Rico a slice it seemed he was still licking the icing off Megan's fingers.

Alpha then glanced around the huge ballroom and her gaze settled on Riley's cousin Zane. He was leaning against the wall and staring hard at Dr. Channing Hastings, the woman he hadn't wanted Megan to invite.

"What are you looking at, baby?" Riley asked her.

She smiled up at him. "Your cousin Zane and how he's staring at Channing Hastings. She's beautiful."

Riley nodded. "Yes, Channing is beautiful both in and out. She and Zane had an affair a couple of years back when she lived here in Denver."

"Now she's engaged to be married to the man with the roving eyes. I bet he's checked out every single woman here today, even a few married ones."

Riley nodded, looking over at the man at Channing's side "You noticed that, as well? She deserves better, which has me wondering why Channing is marrying the guy. I bet Zane is wondering that, as well. But as far as I'm concerned, when you snooze, you lose, and Zane was definitely snoozing when it came to Channing. I would bet any amount of money that he's feeling the pain of his loss. We always warned him that his womanizing ways would cost him one day. So he won't get any pity from me."

Alpha couldn't help but grin. "How can you talk? You were just as much a womanizer."

Riley shook his head. "Nobody could top Zane when it came to women. And, as far as I'm concerned, you have to admit that when I met the woman I knew was for me, I had no problem making her mine and putting a ring on her finger," he said, reaching out and taking her ringed hand in his. "Zane was too stubborn to do that. And I hate to say it, but he probably has lost the only woman he is capable of loving."

"How sad." She truly meant it. Now that she had Riley, she couldn't imagine not having the person you loved in your life. But she had a feeling, from the way Zane was staring at Channing, that Zane would be changing that soon. Alpha couldn't help wondering why Dr. Hastings would marry a man with wandering eyes.

"I've got to get back," she whispered, before brushing a kiss across his cheeks. "My work isn't completed until I get Megan and Rico off on their honeymoon. I think it's wonderful that they're going to Dubai for two weeks."

"Yes, it is wonderful, isn't it?"

She glanced around at all the Atlanta, Montana and Texas Westmorelands she had met over the past couple of days. The men all favored and the women were ultrafriendly. She felt blessed that she was marrying into such a warm and loving family. She smiled when she glanced over and saw Pam and Dillon with their daughter, who'd been born on Christmas Day. She was definitely a beauty.

She then saw Riley's brother, Bane, whom she had just met earlier that day when he had arrived in town. He was such a handsome man she had to take a second look every time she saw him. Even though he was always smiling, she could detect sadness around his eyes. Now she understood Riley's reasons for not wanting to feel the pain his brother was enduring.

"Alpha?"

She glanced up at Riley. Immediately, he lowered his mouth to hers, swiping any thoughts from her mind and kissing her with a hunger that she couldn't help but reciprocate, capturing her tongue in his and doing all sorts of erotic and scandalous things to it.

Scandalous…

It seeped back into her brain just where they were and what she was supposed to be doing. Dislodging her mouth from his, which wasn't an easy feat, she took a step back and drew in a deep breath. "Has anyone ever told you that you shouldn't mess around with the hired help?" she said playfully.

"No, and I wouldn't listen to them anyway. I have tunnel vision when it comes to you, sweetheart."

He took a step closer to regain the distance she'd put between them, bringing his body to hers. She felt something else he had, an erection that was hard and thick. "I'm going now, and I think you need to stay behind this planter until you get yourself together."

He chuckled. "As long as you're close by, I'll never be together—unless you're sharing my bed. And I've been thinking."

"About what?"

"We've had our one winter's night so what about a summer one?" he asked, leaning down and nibbling her lips.

"Riley…" she whispered in a strained voice, "I do need to get back to the wedding."

"No, you don't," he said, wrapping his arms around her. "Lindsey is a great assistant and has everything under control."

"Megan is going to fire me."

"And I will hire you to plan my wedding," he said as his mouth moved lower to nibble her throat.

"Behave," she said, pulling out of his arms again.

"Only if you promise that as soon as this wedding is over you will meet me at Riley's Station for our own after-wedding party."

She gazed up at him. She had a million things to do, but he was right, Lindsey was a great assistant and Alpha had a fantastic staff. "Okay, I promise."

She quickly moved away but couldn't resist glancing back over her shoulder. She was one lucky woman, and later tonight, when she was through with Riley Westmoreland, he would be convinced he was one lucky man.

* * * * *